MW01230116

Kindle Direct Publishing – Amazon Book

Editor
Marcílio de Freitas

Cover
Lucas Corrêa Cândido Ferreira

Freitas, Marcílio de
Sustainability and Covid-19: Michael's Challenges
September 2022 – 104 pages

Keywords: Michael-sustainability-covid19,
Culture-mankind-nature,
People-family-society,   Education-Amazonia-
religion,
Environmental   injustice-poverty-climate
change

Índice para catálogo sistemático
1. Worldwide Literature: a fictional essay
2. Literature: fiction (Brazil)

To Aristóteles de Freitas (in memoriam)

I request Michael's permission to dedicate this book to a person who was large in size and generosity. He lived for 90 years, but he was only with me during the first 21 years of my life. He was not a teacher, but he knew how to teach the secrets of peaceful and solidary human coexistence. He had hundreds of children – seven of his own and the other adopted –, with whom he maintained a very affectionate and respectful closeness. He loved his wife, children, grandchildren and great-grandchildren, and was very optimistic about the future of us all and of mankind. His travels in time in the history of Brazil and mankind were highly appreciated by us all. I still carry with me the sound and the meaning of his words and tales. Your absence is still felt by me, father.

To Aristóteles de Freitas
My beloved father

Sustainability and Covid-19
Michael's Challenges
Marcílio de Freitas

TABLE OF CONTENTS

1. The wheels of the world
2. Why am I here?
3. Diving into my dreams
4. Mom and Dad, how beautiful you are
5. Grandpa and the covid-19 pandemic
6. Grandpa, how will our future be?
7. My commitments to my family and to mankind
8. I want to get to know Amazonia
9. Amazonas river; life and joy
10. My contribution to sustainability
11. I am very happy with our world
12. I want to share my happiness with everyone
13. We will be together later
14. Good night, Mom, Dad, Grandma and Grandpa
15. Amazonia our love
Recommended reading

1. The wheels of the world

People invent the material and symbolic representations that move the world, in all places and at all moments. These people, similar in their mental, emotional and physical structures, seek happiness and noble meanings for their futures, in different ways. They create new commitments, collective projects and universal meanings for human existence, in the construction of a world for everyone. Differences in beliefs, languages and nationalities don't hinder the construction of this civilizing level. They present new problems for those who care about the future of mankind. Potentializing what unites us, valuing our cultures and solidary relationships in family and society are the presuppositions and attributes necessary for the construction of this more equitable world towards sustainability. The role of sustainability in the world and the role of the world in sustainability depend on these social dynamics – that cannot be guided by fear, hatred, exclusion and denial of people. Mankind is being confronted by a new historical responsibility: to build and incorporate socio-economic enterprises into the notion of sustainability, from a perspective that dignifies and values the human condition. Combating social and economic inequality, promoting the ecological preservation of the planet and creating food and health security policies that reach all people are challenges for us and for future generations.

Intervention of societies in this process will make it possible to consolidate situated and localized sustainable development, relativizing it to the historical conditions of each people. This conjuncture will embrace new experiential and cultural perspectives for mankind during the 21st century.

Covid-19 has placed new elements in this picture. By April 2020, more than a third of the world's population has been carrying out social distancing in their homes due to covid-19. These people have been exercising, reflecting, dialoguing, resting, working and reading and creating art. They have also been meditating, praying and planning their futures from an optimistic and hopeful perspective. People and the world are undergoing changes that will improve societies and our relationships with the environment. Soon, covid-19 will be defeated and controlled and new lights will illuminate our lives and mankind.

Rapid reduction of greenhouse gas emissions, environmental destruction and the growing number of unemployed and pauperized people during the covid-19 pandemic have stimulated the implementation of sustainable social and economic programs. To innovate, enterprise, preserve, include and love are the key verbs that will lead to a sustainable future for mankind and the planet.

2. Why am I here?

September 24, 2020. I looked in all directions, quickly identified the scent of people and nature. I reached out and was touched by the people close to me. My thoughts traveled the world.

My thoughts traveled the world. They crossed the Africa of our most ancient ancestors; Europe – the cradle of science and technology – and Asia, which taught us the true meaning of culture. They reached Australia, which has shown mankind the beauty and importance of multiculturalism. They also traveled through America – so generous and solidary and promising. I breathed deeply and experienced different flavors, all still unknown to me. I heard sounds with various intensities and meanings, and I selected those that seemed most important to me. Happiness, love, tolerance, peace and solidarity were chosen. For reasons I don't know, my thoughts control my desires and overflow randomly over everyone and everything around me. I fix my gaze on the stars and let myself travel through the musical flow that radiates in all directions, involving those who are in its reach. A flow that quickly turns into a musical wave that embraces the planet, carrying happiness and hope. I share this event being there and here simultaneously. I am happy with the presence of all of you, here and there. Believe me, I travel, talk, listen, feel, smile, tolerate, respect, am compassionate – and I share my optimism as to a better future for everyone. I have already made my choice. From today on, I will make happiness my instrument for transforming the world, and my work as a way of improving people's quality of life. I place a prism in front of me and identify the spectrum of colors, the rainbow overflowing on the horizon. It illuminates and colors my thoughts and the images that move and give life to the actors and musicians who create and represent their arts, and to the workers and artisans who create humanistic products and art. It also reaches the teachers and students who share lessons and teachings on the history of matter and mankind, and the entrepreneurs who lead innovative enterprises. These lights overflow over religious people who believe in divine justice; over politicians who believe in the common good; and over human beings who cry out and fight for justice. I am here, this is my place. I want to share my happiness with all people. Our differences are not obstacles to sharing a promising and fraternal future for mankind. I must travel in my dreams to create myself and better know my wisdom, so as to share it with everyone.

3. Diving into my dreams

I walk on the clouds looking at places, people, fauna and flora. I identify rivers, forests, plantations, towns, cities, geographies, religions, economies, educational institutions, different galaxies and conceptions of world creation. I talk with the gods about life, religions and the sacred places of the universe. I clarify with them human meanings and beliefs, and mankind's origins and common destiny.

Together, we smile at the beauty of the universe and the fraternal relationships between people and nations. We also talk about politicians and entrepreneurs who must be more humane. We conclude that hell does not yet exist, it is a part of very distant temporal projections... I collect all the heavens with their contents and keep them in a jute bag that is delivered to my mother... I dive into the oceans and am welcomed by its inhabitants – and involved by the plasticity and fleetingness of its forms and colors. I feel I am an inseparable part of these seas that move our origins and climates. I talk with mermaids, algae, fish, and finally with animals and aquatic plants, and am fascinated by the beauty of the cycles of their lives. I am surprised and delighted by the desire of these aquatic beings to also take on human form, to teach the secrets of their wisdom to mankind... In a quick gesture I gather all the oceans and other living beings, and safely shelter them in a small box that I give to my father... Similar to the images in Steven Spielberg's film "E.T. the Extra-terrestrial", I continue my journey pedaling a bicycle that travels in a beam of light, crosses towns, villages, cities, countries, and continents. I talk to people, workers, bosses, religious leaders, politicians, children, the elderly, students, and artists. We smile together when we plan our future; there is no place for lamentation. Food, education, health, housing, transportation, arts, philosophy, mathematics, culture, religion, economy, science and technology, love and peace were the most debated topics. I got to know the foundations of Western culture from France, its welcoming and organized rural areas. Paris and its boulevards, museums and gardens, and its city of science. Its multicultural architecture and customs are so present in our daily life. I have found that the vulgarization of the important issues of our civilization creates insurmountable barriers between men and between nations. Discriminatory and ethnocentric barriers of the West-East type; North-South; poor-rich; developed-underdeveloped; advanced-backward and responsible-irresponsible, typical of colonialist processes. As if there were only two kinds of worlds: that of poor countries and that of rich countries. In the East, I learned other civilizing concepts, with different attributes in quality and quantity. I learned that the philosophy of Eastern peoples has a strong commitment to the temporal dimension, in the form of cycles, in hierarchical order, and of a non-mechanicist nature. The prevalence of a praxis oriented towards the quest for peace, harmony, religious magic and total integration into nature in Eastern culture is replaced by pragmatism, rationalism and technique in our Western culture. I have considered the need to create a new humanistic and holistic concept, privileging the "human condition" integrated into the indivisible world. I come to the African continent of rites and myths, matrices of its cosmogonies, concepts of the world, musicalities and liberation processes. I am thrilled to get to know the cradle of mankind and its more than six hundred peoples and three hundred languages, and one of the world's greatest biodiversity. I look at myself and also recognize myself as an African person; the legacy of Africa's contribution to the historical and cultural construction of the Americas. Tropicality and African joys invade my heart, and transport me, instantly, to the Australian universe, the newest continent in colonial geography. I visit countless islands in the region – great natural environments and social diversity –, finding out about their stories and social integration programs. I participate in their rites and ceremonies and share the ancestral knowledge of the peoples of the region. America, Europe, Asia and Australia are hostage to my desire to imprison them in the purse of my grandmother, where they will remain immobilized by the passing of time... The bag, the box and the purse kept, in order, by my Mom, my Dad and my Grandma no longer communicate directly with each other, leaving mankind divided and isolated between the celestial, terrestrial and aquatic worlds. My transcendental and simultaneous presence in these three worlds puts me in a privileged situation to propose fruitful alternatives to this same mankind... I miss my parents, and have an uncontrollable desire to be physically with them. I leave my state of deep sleep and concentrate on the materialization of their presence.

4. Mom and Dad, how beautiful you are

The process of creation denies destruction. My ability to be everywhere and think for everyone brings me again to my parents. Mom and Dad, how beautiful you are. Dad talks to the murmurs of nature, moves with the lightness of thought and caresses me, hypnotizing me with his gaze. Mom transmits safety, health, love and happiness. I've taken you on my travels, but the desire to know universes and cultures has kept me away. You also take me on your travels – however, my observations and worldly findings are individual.

I feel tenderness and protection when we are together, but what I most appreciate are the love and the responsibility you show toward me. I commit to honor you forever. I have been announced. I always share this sensitivity, comfort and trust in our interpersonal relationships and with people all over the world. You educate me and free me from feelings of injustice and bitterness. Lights, forms, contents, times, spaces, inventions, knowledge, needs and human feelings are priorities that I must quickly understand and apprehend. I need this kind of education to participate in the process of re-creation of the world from the generous perspective that you have taught me. When I look at you, I say to myself: how beautiful my parents are. I love you. Through my mental lens, I see that the covid-19 pandemic has spread throughout the world, causing much sadness and pain. I must talk to Grandpa.

5. Grandpa and the covid-19 pandemic

Grandpa, I have created my own time. It is elastic and different from the time of people's history. I have seen that covid-19 has spread around the world, killing people and destroying families. It is a weapon that victimizes everyone within its reach. It is the negation of life. Grandfather, it has never been more necessary to accelerate the world towards sustainability, in all its dimensions and everywhere. Life is the main heritage from the gods and from parents. People have always been afraid of death. When I travel in a timeline that is not linked to the events and phenomena controlled by the before-after, I see no impediments, in hypothesis, to project the continuity of life after biological death. But science still has no proof or mechanisms to control this scenario. Grandfather, the archangels exist. I have already asked them to help science in this difficult time in which covid-19 continues to threaten the families and the future of mankind. They have a long tradition of controlling and fighting the forces of evil. The entanglement of the actions of the homo sapiens and heavenly forces will make mankind stronger and more determined to combat this new pandemic. We will be together with archangels Michael, Raphael and Gabriel in this long battle against covid-19. Science will eliminate the physical evils this virus can cause to our biological system, and the archangels will protect our hope and spirituality at all times. They will always guide us in the direction of good.

Grandfather, leaders should also summon the poets, artists and musicians, physicists, biologists, chemists and mathematicians to this war against covid-19 that involves the whole of society. Poets understand the essence of life; artists and musicians will humanize this evil entity; and the other four experts have long traditions in solving fundamental problems of matter's atomic and molecular properties. They create the patterns of collective behavior and the profiles of the spirits of these physical entities that form matter, objects and biological life. Together with physicians and mathematicians, they will quickly create analytical models to predict the tendencies of the spiritualized behaviors of atoms and molecules within this evil entity called covid-19. These experts would help solve new strategies to combat this pandemic, in the genesis of its functioning and in its chaotic and global behavior.

Grandpa tells me that, according to health experts, by the end of 2023, covid-19 will be fully controlled in developed countries through vaccination and measures restricting people's mobility. He says that there are still many uncertainties about this picture. The future damage of this virus to people's physical, neurological and spiritual health still challenges scientists and historians. Grandpa emphasizes that the ability of this virus to teleport, its continuous genetic metamorphoses and epidemiological potency in illness of people, and in contamination of the environments must be combated by all humans and non-humans. I insist with my grandfather that – for this world battle – scientific and religious practices and guidelines must be integrated and interwoven in the mind and heart of each person.

I am very apprehensive. The fragility of national health systems in the fight against covid-19 during 2020 and 2021 has demonstrated the managerial incompetence of several national leaders in promoting health safety in their countries. It also has shown, grandfather, that people's health is not separate from their surroundings of conviviality, labor, their family, religion, food, and especially love for others. Most leaders don't have public educational programs for the welfare of children when they are at home. This is expensive and takes a lot of time from public power. This is another drama of the world that has been transformed into a great market led by the leaders.

Grandpa, the privatization of people's health is one of the great tragedies of this century. People's health is considered merchandise. The lack of adequate equipment, secure structures and logistics for health workers and patients, the technical ignorance about the life cycle of the virus, and the lack of an effective medication to combat it have led to many uncertainties concerning its full control.

Its rapid spread and the high probability of illness in the infected patient stimulated social distancing, in all countries, with few exceptions. Grandfather, this set of problems, aggravated by the economic inequality of a large part of mankind, continues to challenge politicians and leaders in different countries. Rich nations should lead the construction of a global solution. All human lives are equally important. My beloved grandfather: the miseries of Africa, and in various nations of the Americas and Asia, have also been built by European countries, especially during the colonial periods. Grandpa, the world is beautiful and indivisible. I was also surprised and concerned about the problems arising from the paralysis of the means of transport and the closing of national borders, in recurrent form. The reduction of public services and the partial operation of most national and transnational productive arrangements have aggravated this social and economic picture. I realize that the social and economic impacts of this new world framework have not yet fully been measured by the experts. Globally, as of March 2022, there have been 450.23 million confirmed cases of covid-19, including 6.02 million deaths, reported to World Health Organization, WHO. In this same period, a total of 10.7 billion vaccine doses have been administered. It has impacted more than 15% of the world's gross product. Grandpa, I believe that these official statistics are inaccurate and unreliable. The global picture is much worse. The contamination of people by covid-19 does not stop growing. In March 2022, the United States, India and Brazil maintained the world leadership in covid-19 contamination and deaths. The pain and suffering caused to people by this pandemic is a great tragedy for mankind. Grandfather says that mankind's critical moment is a unique opportunity for a predatory capitalist economy to redefine its foundations and operational mechanisms. It cannot continue to be centered on exacerbated profit over mankind's basic needs, but on demands of the complementary elements to the social promotion of individuals and societies. In this way, the basic conditions for full civil rights would be assured for everyone, and the complements would depend on people's choices. Education, health, housing, and employment are fundamental rights of every citizen. The world's children would be saved and better protected with love and existential care.

Grandfather says that, in many places, tragicomic situations have occurred during the covid-19 pandemic – such as the case of many husbands lamenting that their wives have been infected in beauty salons, and of wives saying that their husbands have returned infected from their fisheries in isolated places. People have been stoned for being contaminated. Social distancing had led to many divorce requests. The rapid growth in the consumption of alcohol in this period has resulted in increasing depression. The mother who asked the police to bring home her son who was drinking with friends in a bar. The prime minister of a rich country who was hospitalized due to contamination by covid-19 after denying its existence. The drunk and married man who slept with a prostitute contaminated by covid-19. The racist leaders who disclosed that covid-19 only liked African and Asian people. The rulers of several countries who stated that working is more important than living. The son who imprisoned his mother at home to prevent her from leaving, so as to meet his lover contaminated by covid-19. The abandonment of refrigerated trucks with dozens of dead by covid-19 in public places. The revolt of the birds for being accused of transmitting covid-19 to humans and, finally, the return of the superheroes with masks, soap and alcohol gel to help combat covid-19.

For a few moments, I stood looking at my grandfather without knowing what to do. I stopped my laugh, not to embarrass him. But then I spoke up. Grandfather, covid-19 has contaminated the whole world since December 2019. China, the cradle of this damning disease, and South Korea have controlled its spread. Israel and England, after extensive vaccination campaigns, have also managed to control its spread. Gradually, these countries have returned to their full social and economic routines. This reinforces our hopes. Meanwhile, all countries are on alert. Its have presented several cycles of recurrent contamination in regions that have been quickly isolated. Since March 2020, this pandemic is in a rapid process of global expansion. Japan's deadly statistics are still unpredictable. The events that precede the Olympic Games between July 23 and August 8, 2021 in Tokyo took place without an audience – another deleterious requirement of the financial market. India, the world's second most populous country, has intensified social distancing in its various regions. The death statistics in this country are also frightening. Its precarious health system, lifestyle and the high degree of poverty of its population contribute to this nefarious situation. India societies' resistance to following official recommendations aggravates this social framework. By February 2022, this country had recorded some forty-two million infections and five hundred thousand deaths due to covid-19. Numbers that keep growing. Russia has also been hit by covid-19. The difficulty of their leaders in implementing social distancing stimulates the spread of this pandemic and the growing number of deaths. The impacts of covid-19 in its economic and social structure are still very unpredictable. Its global economic isolation due to its recent war against Ukraine amplifies its technical difficulties in fighting this pandemic. Ukraine's situation is desperate. War and covid-19, simultaneously, in its territory, form a desperate social and economic framework and much suffering for its population. Europe, still stunned, is trying to reorganize its health and welfare systems to minimise the number of deaths. Italy, Spain, France and England lead the statistics of deaths by covid-19 in this region. Normality of their social and economic activities integrated with the European community's agreements is still being organized. Full vaccination of their populations is still a distant dream for several European countries. The Americas have also been greatly affected by covid-19.

Since March 2020, Brazil has been in a growing situation of contamination and death by covid-19. Its health and social care system is in full collapse with increasing dehumanization of its public policies. Its citizens are increasingly desperate and frightened – and have little hope for a better future. The death rate of Brazil's contaminated populations continues to rise without sanitary control. From March 2020, Brazil has been in a growing situation of contamination and mortality. Its statistics are frightening. There are more than twenty-nine million two hundred and fifty thousand people infected and six hundred and fifty-four thousand dead by covid-9 until March 2022. After a period of collapse of its health care system, its number of infected and dead by covid-19 has decreased, although cyclically. However, its citizens are still frightened and desperate for a better future. The 163 indigenous peoples of Brazilian Amazonia are in a rapid process of contamination by covid-19. Religious sects, squatters, prospectors and loggers continue to invade their lands and contaminate them with covid-19. The future of these peoples is very uncertain because they are not being adequately protected by the Brazilian president. This pandemic has reached Canada since January 2020. A growing number of contamination and deaths have occurred in their most populous provinces. Covid-19 has also transformed Ecuador into a social and economic chaos. In Guayaquil, coffins with dead people have been abandoned on the streets and in homes. This situation tends to get continuously worse. The African continent has also been contaminated by covid-19. Its lack of social and economic infrastructure makes it difficult to construct more realistic statistics, but its fragile public policies favor the spread of this pandemic in the short term. This situation has been aggravated by natural disasters in the region, such as floods and locust pests. The social scenarios predicted for this region are dramatic and frightening.

On December 8, 2020, Margaret Keenan, a UK grandmother, became the first person in the world to be vaccinated against covid-19. By May 2021, about 1.24 billion people in the world had received at least one dose of the covid-19 vaccine. However, the slow vaccination process and the small supply of vaccine doses by laboratories have hampered the immunization process. Poor countries have been the most fragile, with the highest mortality rates due to covid-19. There is another aggravating factor: several more lethal mutations of covid-19 have appeared in different places around the world. This situation has brought new health and clinical concerns to specialists who investigate its solutions.

Grandpa, I see that mankind's future is still very fragile. By May 2021, the arrogant leaders who favored the economy by denying the mortality power of covid-19, and thus postponed social distancing, had had more deaths in their countries. This has occurred with the United States, England, Japan, Sweden, and continues to happen in Brazil and India.

Grandfather, the impact of covid-19 in the United States has been dramatic and paradigmatic. More than seventy-nine million, four hundred thousand people affected and nine hundred and sixty-four thousand died from this virus, as of

March 2022. Currently, in April 2022, there is a tendency for this health situation to stabilize. It is the country with the highest number of deaths from covid-19 in the world. A national and worldwide shame. Immediately, its leaders must radically change their health protocols and systems, at all levels of social assistance. America is a great country. Its youth needs to have better social protection, and a more humanized and committed education through collective projects. The current President of the United States is mobilizing all American society and public and private structures to reverse this tragic picture. Joe Biden promised that by December 2021 every American person will have been vaccinated against covid-19. Grandfather, the time-history of a generation is very short. All changes are urgent and must include people's social promotion looking to the future. Scientists must urgently invent new strategies to neutralize this type of virus. I understand that covid-19 is treacherous and suicidal. It is transmitted and reproduces quickly and intriguingly kills its own host, determining its own death. Somehow its genes are organized to, when possible, destroy the genetic structure of human cells.

But grandfather, please explain to me how covid-19 acts in the human body? Covid-19 is transmitted by droplets in the air, due to the coughing and sneezing of infected people. It can also be transmitted through physical contact with contaminated solid surfaces. In general, its doors in our organism are the nasal mucous membranes, the eyes and the mouth. After entering our organism, covid-19 invades human cells and, under favorable physical-chemical conditions, multiplies rapidly, in the form of clones of itself.

My dear grandson, the biological basis of the human organism is an open physical system. It is fully integrated and connected between itself and the external environment. In a continuous way, the human organism exchanges mass and energy among itself and the external world. But, going back to covid-19: science has already shown that as this virus reproduces in the human body; it presses on the cell walls until it breaks them, spreading its infected content and its clones. These clones, in turn, invade and sicken new cells in a fast and continuous process.

Coughing, fever, severe respiratory deficiencies, lung infections, pneumonia and paralysis of several organs are biological complications that can overcome a person's immune system and cause death. This process of illness has spread across the world, increasing the flow of patients who need hospitalization, and thus overloading and collapsing health systems. Experts know the target of the disease, its possible location in the environment, its transmission form and its power of destruction. This information is essential but still insufficient for the construction of a vaccine for the immunization of people on a large scale. Research groups, in global networks, carry out continuous and persistent work with this objective. Hollywood filmmakers are having a rich worldwide cultural collection to reinvent their fiction films. There is no news of a superhero with covid-19. Certainly they are in full social distancing. Grandpa, but does this virus have a spirit? Yes, grandson, it has the spirit of evil, of darkness, of destruction of life.

Grandfather, I have another concern. Not all religions clarify whether animals have a spirit or not. I believe in the existence of spirituality of animals. Religions must perform a worldwide exorcism to expel covid-19 from the planet and imprison it in the prisons beyond. This ecumenical action is urgent. The distancing of people and the isolation of countries and continents in the fight against covid-19 have strengthened reflection and family cohesion. However, the economic conditions of people and countries have been continuously deteriorating. At this conjuncture, leaders and international economic institutions are responsible for solving all the financial problems that collectively threaten human lives. The partnership with society will ensure the joint construction of better social and economic alternatives for the well-being of everyone, now and in the future. Grandpa, there is no individual way out of this dramatic crisis.

Grandpa: although our lives are fragile and fleeting, the gods and our families want us alive. Nobody wants to die, and everyone intends to enter heavenly paradise after their definitive departure from Earth. Just as people continue to avoid agglomerations, always cleaning their hands and using masks to avoid contamination by covid-19, it is necessary that the divine and supreme powers purify the Earth, including also all its animal, plant and mineral kingdoms – and that they show different illuminated paths to those who have already departed into other celestial dimensions, blessing them in their new initiations and realizations. New connections are being created between the celestial and terrestrial worlds. Grandpa, my generation will actively participate in the emerging sustainability of this new world.

Grandpa agrees with me. The world has changed radically with the great social and economic crisis that will persist during this decade.

I believe that this conjuncture shows the need for mankind to rethink and change several foundations of its routine, the organization of societies and its productive matrices. The rapid and planetary spread of covid-19 and its new genetic variants, the different dynamics of contagion and illness of people by covid-19 in different countries, and the difficulty in organizing a synchronized worldwide management in the fight against it all prevent the construction of a technical and political protocol for a unified global response. Grandfather, these features of covid-19 favor its recurrence on a large scale due to the international mobility of people and travelers infected or already immunized to the virus.

I realize that people's suffering, pain, fear and concern have occupied all the spaces and times in the world. But the opportunity to tread new paths and challenges has motivated these same people to create a sustainable world. The sad and joyful memories are important subjective tools for incorporating sustainable practices into my relationship with covid-19. I will use the sad ones to weaken them and the joyful ones to neutralize their pandemic effects and minimize the suffering of marginalized populations.

Grandfather, while traveling through time, I anticipate three possible great scenarios for these relationships. But I remind you that this virus was not generated in underdeveloped countries. The first scenario considers that the probability of reducing the flow of virus to acceptable levels simultaneously in all countries is very small. This issue poses long-term social, economic and diplomatic problems for all countries, with greater impacts for the underdeveloped. Grandpa, unfortunately several public policies in these countries have been in the process of collapse, chaos and barbarism. Many people have died and others are dying without medical assistance. Together with the archangels, I note that a wave of pain and suffering has embraced the entire planet. Gods have extended a sacred mantle of purification over animal and plant lives. New hopes and spiritualities have emerged.

Grandpa, the second tendency of these relations, similar to other pandemics, foresees the continued circulation of the virus in our organisms, immunizing them on a large scale, although they will remain carriers of its harms. The dynamics of our coexistence with this new host is still an unknown factor that leads to future concerns. Slow and continuous control over this disease will allow populations to adapt to their new routines and to the re-signification of public policies. Leaders' interventions directed at people's social and economic inclusion, international solidarity and a new spiritual perspective for the world will be present in this scenario.

Grandfather, finally, there is a third scenario in which the virus would be controlled by means of a specific vaccine to be applied on a large scale. The full concreteness of this latter scenario, the safest for public policies in health, is unclear until 2023. But there have been several mutations of the virus, altering its potency of contamination and death of people. The health implications of the growing vaccination process that is taking place in several countries still must be evaluated. Laboratory tests have shown that this virus undergoes mutations that make it more infectious and more lethal. Another alternative would be the invention of a specific medication to increase people's antibodies and immunity against all possible variants of the virus.

My dear grandson, science will triumph over covid-19. Many medical research groups have partnered with the pharmaceutical industry to improve the vaccine, other medications and combat the psychosomatic effects of this pandemic.

Grandpa, the problem is that, again, poor African communities can be used as guinea pigs for this type of research. This needs to be denounced and combated by everyone. This pandemic is stimulating prejudice and racism everywhere. Grandpa, we have to be very careful that social injustices are not amplified in this difficult period of mankind.

However, the covid-19 pandemic is no impediment to structuring social changes. George Floyd's death in a violent racist police approach in May 2020 in the city of Minneapolis caused the explosion of hundreds of anti-racist manifestations in major world cities. The US police's security system has been put under pressure by society and is under review in several American states.

My dear grandfather, after reflecting on these scenarios I present my conclusions about the consequences of covid-19. The most dramatic consequence is the destruction of life. Others that touch me are its impacts on our fictional imagery, our routines, and on politics, economy, science and education. A change of worldview is ongoing – to a new world that values solidary social practices, inclusive public policies and the environmental protection of the planet. Social distancing and isolation, and lockdowns in cities and countries will become cyclical, according to the degree of dissemination and mortality of pandemics and the economic interests of financial elites. Leaders' political hypocrisy has become a powerful weapon against the most socially and economically vulnerable people. In the poorest regions, the degree of lethality of covid-19 will reach absurd proportions. Grandpa, I believe that fascist leaders are allowing this pandemic to eliminate large swathes of economically vulnerable people. Their public policies don't protect these people, and lead to their contamination and death.

Grandpa, on the other hand, the form of organization and deliberation of political parliaments, public managers and economic systems and platforms have incorporated structural innovations. These innovations have radically changed the flows of decisions and functioning of parliaments, societies and markets on a global scale. Changes in the forms of production and circulation of capital require new forms of fiscal and tributary control in productive arrangements and a lowering of wages for a large portion of workers in the world. Soon, I will lead a major global social movement against the oppression of politics and the market.

Grandpa, the fight against covid-19 has taught people that their routines cannot be held hostage by politicians and the market. Our innocence, values and courage, and perseverance and sense of justice have been continually transgressed by these social agents because of their spurious interests. Grandfather, the red, blue and yellow primary colors must continue illuminating and distributing more love, hope and prosperity to the world. Now, I better understand the limits of science and technology's response to issues related to our survival. Doctors and scientists don't perform miracles, they are humans, and have also been victims of covid-19. They have worked tirelessly to invent the vaccine against this virus in a world threatened by death and also by the suffering caused by wars and hunger. Children's joys and singers' songs have been drowned out by the pain and suffering of the infected. Thousands of families mourn the loss of loved ones in a war against an invisible enemy that occupies territories preventing people's movements and isolating them in closed environments.

Grandfather, welcome to my fantasy world. Now we are getting to know each other, talking about all the concerns of our family and mankind. We have been playing a lot and talking about our future. There is no consensus among us.

On the other hand, grandson, we are witnessing the anticipation of several structural changes that were already ongoing. Grandpa highlights the world's virtualization, distance education, remote work and the form of organization of public policies, societies, national states and also economic groups that have taken on greater social responsibility. Grandfather states that these changes have been permeated by sustainability. Grandpa also warns that, in this pandemic world, the fragility of life and the political and economic regimes in the solution of existential crises of global impact have become evident.

Grandpa, my life is changing in this brief time of my existence. I am witnessing the review of our beliefs and values prioritizing teamwork and networking, and the re-elaboration of our consumption habits and human impacts on nature. I participate in the restructuring of the consumer society, reaffirming only its aspects that contribute to social promotion. I note that people are more anxious and concerned about health care and private and collective environments avoiding places with large agglomerations. The businesses are developing new strategies to ensure a sense of security in the workplace and entertainment. Stores, bars, restaurants, bookstores, shops, gyms, schools, universities have redesigned their spaces and operating methodologies to reduce agglomerations and facilitate the offer of its services and products.

Grandfather, to me all this change is novelty. Personal hygiene logistics has been available to all citizens. New business models have been offered to customers. Delivery services and immersive experiences have grown significantly. Great impacts occurred in the cultural industry, especially in the online shows, in mass sports and in tourist visits and virtual bibliographic consultations through robotics and available cybernetic technologies. I have never been to a restaurant. I only know about them through the internet. Remote work has been intensified through cybernetic environments connected to local and global networks, expanding sales on the internet, distance learning with online courses and new learning platforms with different approaches on specific topics.

Grandfather, I repeat that the dynamics of public and private productive arrangements and the social distancing to large parts of national societies are very dependent on the duration and evolution of these scenarios. The secondary effects of covid-19 on our health are also worrying. A more humanized globalization committed to the future of people and the planet will emerge in this new civilizing process. I don't believe that people change instantly. But, after this crisis, we will have more elements to create a better world.

Grandfather, I imagine that this pandemic has resulted in new forms of behavior and habits. The fight against it has led to new methodologies for planning and organizing companies and economic groups. It has demanded the continuous hygiene of the body, home and environments, new feeding practices as well as more flexible and fair forms of working relationships, using convergence technologies and new methods of large-scale distance learning. Grandfather, I am taking classes on the internet. My school is rethinking the forms, contents, and operational mechanisms of its educational programs. It is preparing to form citizens of the world, with technical skills but also committed to people and mankind.

Grandpa tells me that the pandemic's resurgence has triggered a set of preventive measures. He highlights the following: the systematic control over infected people, less flow of cars, people's mobility, labor in alternating shifts, implementation of several income transfer programs and the prohibition of major events. He also highlights the operation of sanitary control posts in strategic urban and rural places, and the intensification of use of information and communication platforms.

Grandpa tells me that organized societies have pressured the international institutions and leaders of developed countries for the creation of specific economic funds to accelerate social and economic inclusion in underdeveloped countries. These same societies have also demanded high investments in improving public health, especially in bioindustry and pharmacology. Grandfather emphasizes that the industry has directed large investments in the research in physics and chemistry of new materials prioritizing the sectors of health, education, transport, housing, food and culture. Grandpa also clarifies that more regulations for greater control of deforestation and the use of fungicides and pollutant emissions, at all levels and places, have been demanded. According to my grandfather, it is necessary to improve the quality of life of people and nature.

Grandfather also tells me that human life is very dependent on nature, and insists on the need for the environmental education of all people – from a perspective in which families, communities, societies, national states, and international institutions develop new programs and methodologies for nature preservation. Grandpa explains that new proposals to improve the relationship between humans and nature are being implemented, prioritizing housing, mobility, circulation, employment, labor, social centers, productive arrangements, platforms of public policies and international cooperation, and climate change. Through Grandpa's teachings, I realize that sustainability emerges in all its splendor, in different intensities and contexts.

Grandfather, the social distancing of the world's populations and the paralyzation of trade's wide sectors and global industry have helped the world to rethink its forms of coexistence and organization. Official statistics project that world trade in 2020 and 2021 will retract by more than 15%, with major impacts on globalized social and economic structures. I believe that our family will have no difficulty integrating into the new world that will be born after the control of this pandemic.

Grandpa, valuing health systems and public education is an immediate requirement. I also believe that changing the concept and the sense of economic development, and re-signifying several cycles of productive arrangements are emerging challenges. Grandfather, these changes start with our basic needs: food, health, housing, education, productive arrangements, labor, urban mobility, entrepreneurship, leisure, and religion. Love, solidarity, freedom, fraternity, joy, pleasure, preserving, and sharing are the fuels of these changes, involving cultural, demographic, economic and geographical elements of countries, and continents.

Grandfather: in my magic mirror I can see that you have lived through many pandemics since the Black Plague in the Middle Ages. So, I listen to your considerations with great attention and apprehension. Grandfather also says that there has been a relationship between the emergence of epidemics and pandemics with the world food chain. He claims that our forms of feeding have contributed to the generation of major epidemics in this century. Ebola started in Africa, swine flu in Mexico, avian influenza in Hong Kong, mad cow disease in the UK, and covid-19 in Wuhan are pandemics due to the handling of animals used for food.

The main sources of these pandemics are associated with serious failures in the organization of various food chains. Grandpa highlights the obtaining of food from the carcasses of wild animals, and the large-scale rearing of chickens imprisoned and contaminated by feces in small cages. He also mentions the creation of pigs confined on an industrial scale and subjected to a continuous process of stress, and oxen fed on animal feed unsuitable for human use. Although the causes of some of them are still completely unknown, inadequate food and inappropriate sanitary conditions in environments and people have a strong presence in these evils of mankind. Grandpa, this pandemic is a social construct.

Grandfather, the destruction of the natural habitats of animals and birds, smuggling, commercialization and consumption of these animals, in rural and urban communities, have increased the spread of the diseases transmitted by bacteria and viruses. The creation and industrialization of the animals and birds on a large scale without proper sanitary control, and the agriculture in large tropical territorial areas with the uncontrolled use of fungicides and herbicides have aggravated this situation. Grandfather, I have been talking a lot with the birds and the animals. They are very sad and scared by the destruction of nature. You can imagine the regional and global impacts resulting from the cultural and ecological destruction of Brazilian Amazonia. This region has 5 million km², more than 163 cultures, 400 billion trees and 2,000 rivers. How many woes and diseases could be spread to the world? An announced tragedy is ongoing.

My generation is very apprehensive about covid-19 and our social distancing. I believe that, for people's better safety, national leaders and organised society must reevaluate the functioning of the global food and beverage industry chain. This industry prioritizes profit over the quality of sanitary conditions, and the food safety of the population. But Grandpa, world food security is another human tragedy. Hungry people need access to food. Today there are more than 800 million people who don't eat properly, a large amount of them concentrated in the world's poorest regions. Grandpa, the institutions that finance the world's economic development have no interest in solving this problem. It is not profitable. Covid-19 has aggravated the social framework that also contributes to the planet's environmental destruction.

Grandpa clarifies that a healthier life for mankind also depends on the sustainability of the global food security policy. Grandpa says that this sustainability requires the social control of the global food chain from its origin, productivity, transportation and storage to its quality, sale and consumption. Grandfather claims that this chain has a strong connection with the destruction of natural environments contributing to climate change. Grandpa tells me that agricultural practices use 75% of the surface fresh water consumed and 33% of the planet's solid surface. And that, also, there is an annual waste of one third of the world's food production, about 1.3 billion tons, which corresponds to the loss of US$ 1 trillion per year. Grandfather, low productivity, continuous concentration of land and the expulsion of small landowners from their production sites by large farmers and food companies contribute to this waste and the production of hunger in communities surrounding large agricultural areas.

Grandfather, economic forces and human activities have changed the dynamics of nature's cycles on Earth. Through windows in time, I realize that predatory capitalism has accelerated this process. Pollution, occupation and disorderly use of territories, great deforestation and burning, extinction of various animal and vegetable species, and the pandemics are social and economic constructions that my generation will have to deconstruct.

Grandpa, mankind is in a new geological age called the "Anthropocene." It needs to be redeemed. The main references of this period are the marks of ecological destruction of the planet by humans, since the industrial revolution. Grandfather, it is also our challenge to create a force of global political cohesion that enables planetary unification with a sustainable future for mankind. My dear Grandfather, how will our future be?

6. Grandpa, how will our future be?

Grandfather, the day after tomorrow is Sunday. What will we do? How will we be? What about the future of mankind and our planet? How will we be in 2050?

Grandfather tells me that he initially talked about this moment and some developments. He reaffirms that covid-19 has been ruthless with mankind, everywhere. Grandpa makes me an important observation. "Mankind has always improved its ethical values throughout its history. In the near future, it will emerge stronger, more qualified and more united from this crisis." I tell Grandpa that the world did not stop during the social distancing of mankind. People were closer to their family members living their new routines and also renewing their dreams and plans for the future. Grandfather affirms that the pandemic has sent the world into recession. The impacts of this virus on the economic and social policies of countries will last this entire decade, with great mortality and suffering in the most impoverished populations of Africa, Asia and Americas. Now, there is no immediate solution to this global health and existential crisis. The definitive solution is the invention of a medication or vaccine that immunizes people as is occurring now. This pandemic will be defeated, despite the slow vaccination process.

Hundreds of millions of people in the world could be saved or immunized quickly against covid-19 if leaders determined the loss of property rights over the manufacturing process of vaccines in use. This "patent break" would enable rapid vaccination on a global scale and would end the suffering and pain of a large part of the world's population. Then we can concentrate our efforts to solve other complex problems of people and mankind. Grandpa reaffirms all the considerations he has already made about covid-19.

Grandpa also declares that this framework strengthens the isolation of regions and countries, the regionalization of productive arrangements, sustainable practices and intensified nationalism and populism. This crisis has highlighted a great contradiction: as the economy becomes globalized, political power remains nationalized. The debate for a world government mediated by organized societies and nationalized and regionalized political structures will be part of the world political agenda after this crisis. The reverse is also feasible. Grandpa, this issue is very important to me. I would like to have several citizenships at the same time. I would be Brazilian, Portuguese, French, German, English, American, Congolese, Chinese, Japanese, Australian, at least. I would be a citizen of the world, in way of thinking and acting, and also in my origins. But you would still be my grandfather. I love you so much.

Grandpa comments that since the beginning of this pandemic the supplies of many arrangements and productive chains necessary for people's survival and well-being have been interrupted. He also emphasizes that the main countries responsible for the supply of this type of input, China and the United States, are meeting, as a priority, their domestic demands. However, he clarifies that China has met the world's highest demands for medical equipment for protection against covid-19. According to Grandpa, there is a concern of Western leaders with the possibility of China becoming the "factory of the world." He says a quick political analysis shows that this framework is likely to happen in the near future. The other countries develop strategies to ensure their participation, in the greatest possible intensity, in different parts of the production chains. China is also part of the select group of countries that have led the manufacture of the covid-19 vaccine.

Grandpa, China is in a privileged position to lead global economic revitalization. It is rapidly recovering from this pandemic and is prepared to deal, if necessary, new waves of covid-19. The intensive use of health technologies, social technologies, cybernetics, robotics and bioindustry in control of covid-19 contributed to its rapid elimination. Unlike other countries, its economy already predicts growth of at least 9% by the end of 2021. The full operation of its industrial matrix and service sector, together with its large domestic consumption market and its structural and logistical capacity for global export of products and services will guarantee a Chinese economic growth of more than 8% in 2022. Certainly, at the end of this decade there is a strong tendency for Chinese Gross Domestic Product to overtake that of the United States of America, becoming the world's largest economy. Grandpa, for this same period I also predict that the rest of the world will still be hostage by a set of political and economic uncertainties typical of combating the covid-19 virus. Its health policy to combat covid-19 has revealed a new China to the world. European and American politicians are frightened and frightened by the scientific and technological development of this millennial country. China is in the process of transition to lead the high-tech public policy market on a global scale. The way in which the Chinese authorities have integrated technological innovations into their health policy to combat covid-19 is an example to the world. China is also in the scientific leadership for manufacturing the vaccine against covid-19. Grandpa, you already told me about the "Story of Afanti," the famous Chinese folktale that enchants your children. I believe that soon, the Chinese cartoons recreating the stories of the heroes and the oppressed will be enchanting the Western world in a new civilizing perspective. A perspective that is more integrated into nature and more reflective, but not less oppressive. Universalism idealized by Europeans will be reconstructed from a new Eastern perspective. I also believe that Europe and the United States will form a large political bloc to dispute economic spaces in the new global market led by China. Science, technology, innovation and sustainability will be the fuels of this new world. My beloved grandfather, according to the Chinese leaders, in this new stage of development there will be no hunger nor great social inequalities in China. Grandpa, I am convinced that soon China will have a great influence on the global economy and culture. I hope to learn about China and its cultural heritage.

Grandfather, soon, the re-signification of the categories "life," "freedom," "democracy" and "development" will be incorporated and strengthened in the global political agenda. European, American and Chinese experts will also have a hegemonic role in this process of vital importance for mankind's future. Sustainability will be the fuel of this new global political and economic scenario.

My dear grandson, the world has experienced rapid and radical changes over the last two decades. The classical theories of philosophy and sociology have no theoretical and empirical scope to explain these structuring social and economic changes. Covid-19 has intensified this new ontological and epistemological crisis.

During the period of the fight against covid-19, globalization's main actors continue strengthening and qualifying their economic bases, and expanding their reach. Contradictorily, this feature of globalization has also strengthened politics, considering the growing capacity of organization and mobilization of society. A new framework arising from this context is very dependent on funding for scientific and technological innovations. The moment requires caution in this regard.

Grandfather clarifies that the global social distancing during covid-19 pandemic is a victory of politics, and also of media sectors, on the economy and the market. Countries that have delayed this decision have had the greatest impact of this disease with large numbers of deaths. But contemporary societies continue hostage to the market economy. The game of power between politics and market continues to tend towards the economy. My grandfather emphasizes that the main countries responsible for the supply of this type of input, China and the United States, are meeting, as a priority, their domestic demands.

Grandfather says international tourism has been the economic sector most affected by covid-19.

According to my grandfather, this crisis has quickly "swallowed up" trillions of dollars in global stock exchanges and has led to bankruptcy, millions of small businesses around the world. Immediately, there has been the growth of economic inequality, and the strengthening of clientelist and populist leaders.

On the other hand, the deleterious impacts of this pandemic have contributed to the intensification of international scientific and technological cooperation aimed at combating and eliminating it. They have also made it possible to implement a new occupation matrix centered on the execution of work at home, in the services sector. This pandemic has shown to the world a perverse dimension of developed countries' priorities: their leaders continue the construction of war technologies to the detriment of the strengthening of their public health systems. The pandemic also stimulates class relations by increasing poverty and, at the same time, it has shown the limitations of medical knowledge and practices.

Grandpa, mankind currently has a more realistic radiography of poverty in the world. It has been unraveling, showing the ills of political systems. The leaders hide poverty. They don't like people. I am impressed by the poverty scenarios in Brazil, a country with a population of 210 million people (in 2020). During this pandemic, its aid programmes for the most deprived have identified more than 50 million people in extreme poverty. This social segment has been invisible in official statistics and in mainstream media. This is a major challenge for sustainability in national states and on the planet. At this perverse juncture, doctors and other health workers have saved many lives. They have become heroes of mankind. Grandfather, I want to be a doctor when I grow up.

Certainly, you, Dad and Mom will be very proud of me. I have also noticed that mankind's health crisis will induce changes in people's routine. Lower consumption of superfluous objects, the manufacture of more sustainable products, a less hedonistic and more nationalized fashion market, an education more focused on human values, the intensification of remote work, and greater corporate social responsibility and an economy centered on sustainability are ongoing tendencies. Certainly, the feelings of compassion, faith and hope will be more present in people's lives.

Grandpa says he is very optimistic about mankind's future. Human knowledge and the wisdom accumulated since the beginning of our civilization give us this security. The history of civilizations describes many world tragedies faced by mankind. All these crises have been controlled by it. People have become wiser and more compassionate. Family, societies, and mankind are social and cultural constructions that ennoble our life, now and in the future.

Grandfather, on Sunday, we will be together as a family talking about our relationships, our commitments to you, my parents, and my uncles. We will have lunch with grilled fish and *guaraná* and set our schedule for next week. Grandpa, then we will visit, simultaneously, the Forbidden City in Beijing; the pyramids in Egypt; the Sydney Opera House in Australia; the Parthenon in Athens, Greece, birthplace of Western culture; and Brazilian Amazonia. During breakfast we will travel through the history of mankind, in the different temporal dimensions that imprison these historical references in granny's purse. We will move along the borders of the past and the present, focusing on cultures and on the commitment of peoples to nature and peace. We will talk with Confucius (VI B.C.) about the customs and moral standards in his time; with the philosopher Ptah-Hotep (5000 B.C.) about the culture and wisdom of the Egyptian people; and also with Nelson Mandela (1918-2013) about nature, human virtues and the process of liberation in Africa; with Eddie Mabo (1936-1992) about indigenous rights in Australia; with Plato and Aristotle (IV B.C.) on the matrices of Western civilization; and with Tuxaua Ajuricaba (18st century) about the strategies to resist to colonial domination in Brazilian Amazonia. We will be well, happier, more mature and ready for the next week of work.

Our journey to mankind's future is exciting. The constructs of worldwide realities in 2050 pose uncertainties and complex challenges. When we move along the optimistic timeline, we see the rapid global demographic expansion; 1 billion people in 1830, 2 billion in 1930, 3 billion in 1960, 4 billion in 1975, 5 billion in 1990, 6 billion in 2000, just over 7 billion in 2010, 8 billion by 2025, and more than 9.5 billion by 2050. We certify that this demographic evolution of mankind, in the last two centuries, has generated immediate impacts on its policy of food security, and the use and occupation of the soil. It also impacted its territorial ordering, the use of natural resources, organization of professions, industrial matrices, and the relationships between countries and people and the civilizing process. It has spread human knowledge in all regions and has also contributed to the spread of racism, arrogance, greed, hypocrisy and greed in a perspective in which economic interests have always prevailed.

Grandpa, racism is mankind's worst evil. Nobody is born racist. It is impregnated in the imagination and subjectivity of people as a material and symbolic heritage of our colonial and slavish past. Grandpa, racism is a historical, ideological and social disease that has corrupted our spirits and sociability. It is a type of vírus of darkness that has been incrusted in our consciousness and affectivity since our gestation. It is the negation of material and transcendental life. A cursed heritage that you adults are leaving to my generation. Grandpa, only love does not overcome racism. Politics, the judiciary and the financial market are its main radiating sources. Hollywood and our national constitutions preach freedom as if it could exist in racist political regimes. As long as there is racism, humans will not be fully free. In different ways, racism, like freedom, always involves other people simultaneously. My dear grandfather, the pain and suffering arising from a racist action are also of all the world's citizens. In the same way that there are machines to account daily for all world economic production, there should be a similar structure to register and periodically denounce all racist injustices committed in our countries. Yesterday I spoke with Frederick Douglass, a best-known leader of the abolitionist movement in the United States, during the 19st century.

Douglass was an ex-slave, a leader in the anti-slavery movement and one of the first African-American citizens to defend women's rights. He was outraged when I told him that after 156 years of Promulgation of the Thirteenth Amendment to the American Constitution in 1865, freeing all slaves in the United States, racism continues to be cultivated and promoted in his country. Racism generates hate, social exclusion and the denial of social diversity. There is no vaccine against racism. It is a social construction by people, families, school systems, communication systems, ruling classes and also by national and international institutions. Mankind has had several scientific and technological revolutions and continues to cultivate racism. The complete elimination of racism is an indispensable condition for creating sustainability. Judicial structures and national states must be humanized to better protect social groups and people who are victims of racism. The murder of George Floyd by the police in the USA shows that it denies the right to citizenship to black people. Historically, the global and regional financial elites, governments and systems of repression of national states reproduce and cultivate racism. The explosions of anti-racist manifestations around the world pose challenges for us all: to humanize the structures of national states and to promote social diversity and multiculturalism. This is a long journey for successive generations. Grandpa, I have asked for help from Abraham Lincoln, William Shakespeare, Pablo Neruda and Nelson Mandela to lead a great world movement to eliminate racism from mankind. There is no place for hate in this civilizing challenge. Grandpa, please look at the stars. We are not alone in the universe.

Grandpa, rethinking our habits and customs, our ways of educating young people, planning and organizing public policies and industrial matrices, economic processes, mechanisms of international cooperation and our conceptions of the world are demands of this new epoch.

Grandpa tells me that in 2011 there were about 800 million people living in conditions of undernourishment. The covid-19 pandemic has aggravated this statistic that keeps growing. Today, in 2050, despite the declining population birth rate, poverty still prevails and climate change has intensified with irreversible impacts on the planetary ecology. Unprotected families, abandoned children, world pandemics, climate change, the continuous global economic crises and the delay in the construction of public policies for the planet's environmental protection contributed to this reality. This framework definitively challenged the thesis of continuous and unlimited economic growth based on smoky and unhealthy industrial matrices. The public policies of health protection are ineffective and are hostage to predatory capitalism. Grandfather, this framework you presented is dramatic. Although I remain optimistic, this situation has me worried.

This conjuncture requires creating and travelling through the time of history in an interrupted fight against unsustainable enterprises. Exterminate misery, promote literature, agroecology, renewable energy, bioindustry, nanotechnology, fine chemistry, photonics, quantum electrodynamics, cybernetics, robotics, aerospace and convergence technologies, information and communication technologies, scientific instrumentation of high precision, among others, are necessary initiatives to change this morbid picture. Establishing greater connectivity and interregional convergences by strengthening the processes of social and cultural inclusions and the trends to reduce socioeconomic inequalities with the growth of the use of technological innovations, diversified sources of non-fossil energy, and social programs of solidarity are challenges of this new era of global sustainability. Incorporating the arts and music in all educational matrices poses more critical and human perspectives on these challenges.

In this half of the 21st century, it is necessary to reaffirm the change in the global economic structure towards the economy of information and services, with a reduction in the flow of mass and energy due to the introduction of efficient technologies and clean energy sources. Insist on global solutions for environmental, social and economic sustainability through balanced regional development, investing in the process of reversing the impacts of global climate change. During covid-19, there was a great decrease in planetary air pollution. Fewer cars in the streets, a reduction in industrial activities, social distancing and a decrease in the use of fossil fuels contributed to this situation, which has a strong correlation with climate change. However, after the control of covid-19, air pollution grew again rapidly reaching dangerous levels.

Providing water use and access to food for all, to reduce the incidence of endemic and epidemic diseases, and minimize the use of natural resources and environments due to the need to minimize the predatory process of urbanization and industrialization are public concerns everywhere. Grandpa, creating an economic fund to promote a minimum income program for all impoverished families in the world is one of the greatest political challenges of mankind. Protecting children is a challenge for all of us. An ethical commitment of my generation.

In a broad form, my generation observes similar impacts of ecological depreciation on the continents. It also notes that the leaders have been mobilizing to combat the increase in the planet's average temperature, the loss of biodiversity, the reduction in rainfall and the increase of evaporation with disruptions in the hydrological cycle, and the declines in agricultural and forestry production. There are continuous warnings about the melting of glaciers affecting the degree of acidity in oceanic waters and its food chains, the longer duration of seasons and the intense heat waves that impact human health. Environmental control centers also record an increase in regional differences in the distribution of natural resources, the difficulties of adaptability of organisms due to climate change, and the summers and winters more rigorous. Food security policies have been greatly impacted with less water availability for consumption, agriculture and power generation, the intensification of the process of salinization and desertification of agricultural land, and the reduction of agricultural productivity with adverse consequences for food security policies. The rising levels of oceans, rivers and flooding of the surrounding plains, the negative disturbances in fish stocks and the intensification of tropical tornadoes, acid rain and pollution phenomena also aggravate this dramatic picture. Grandpa, there's still time to build a better world for your great-grandson.

In the civilizing conception defended by my generation, a more spiritualized cosmic genesis must prevail. The universes and the lives that animate it are social constructions and, simultaneously, a blessing from the gods. These heavenly and earthly heritages are an invaluable

45

treasure. Other different conceptions of the world have emerged in the 2050s. National and international institutions are mobilizing themselves to build new mythical and spiritual alternatives aimed at the formation of men and women committed to the planet's perpetuity. There is also the effort of mankind at all levels to incorporate sustainable practices in industrial and occupational matrices, consolidating this type of development centered on environmental and social protection. With joy we note the predominant presence of the arts, philosophy, mathematics, anthropology of techniques, sociology of sciences, linguistics, environmental education, ecotourism, environmental services, recycled products, green economy, bioindustry, clean development mechanisms and solidary public policies, in a sustainable perspective.

Grandpa, the arts are necessary for our physical and spiritual liberation. They liberate people from the bureaucracy and suffocating control of politics and the market. They are the gateway to our cosmic insertion and the main counterpoint to the rules and decaying morality of a civilization centered on individualism and absolute privatization. The arts are the main manifestation of beauty and of the being. For these reasons, they have to be imbricated in all human inventions and innovations. Products and public policies have to be spiritualized. My dear grandfather, adults have lost the ability to feel this important dimension of human life. When they look at the sky they only see the stars and other objects in its movements synchronized with the human clocks. Sometimes science and philosophy dull human minds and hearts.

Increasing the degree of interference of high technologies in public policies aimed at the preservation of the planet and improving the quality of life of its populations is a challenge in all current private and public institutions. Concentrating global efforts on combating poverty, the greenhouse effect, wars, pollution and intolerance among people, creating new perspectives to build more systemic and integrating solutions for mankind's future, reaffirms our commitment to a better world for all.

Grandfather warns that the most important thing is not the confrontation between science and religion. What is under discussion is not the weakening of rationality to the detriment of mysticism, prophecies, fables, curses or theological knowledge – but the convergence of its material and symbolic representations of sciences and religions aim at the improvement of people and the society. Family, life, the universe and love are our most precious legacies. My dear grandson, I love you.

Grandpa, in 2100 we will be together again, witnessing the splendor of life, dignity and social promotion in the world, in continents, in countries, in cities, in communities and also in our families, with no exceptions. In a universe moved by love and solidarity, centered on the perpetuity and the improvement of life. Our descendants will face other challenges and collective responsibilities that are more complex than ours.

7. My commitments to my family and to mankind

My parents told me I still have a lot to learn. However, I am sensitive to the importance of certain material and symbolic contributions to the improvement of mankind.

Sigmund Freud (1856-1939) discovered that the historical and physical reality of the world depends on our psyche, where the matrices of rationality and irrationality of our dreams, fears and desires coexist. Our fantasies, solidarities and commitments to family and mankind are driven by languages that radiate from this psychic base, which makes us unique and universal. No less important is the fusion of the stories of nature with that of mankind. Our manifestations and existential needs are not dissociated from nature's cycles and processes. Air, land, water and various chemical elements that constitute the basis of matter are physical structures of nature inseparable from life. Therefore, our true history moves, simultaneously, several dimensions of civilization that include categories of the type psyche, society, spirituality, matter, nature, life and praxis. Time, space, energy, peace, love, solidarity, among others, constitute the foundations of these categories indispensable to human existence.

Edgar Morin (1921-....) also includes ethics on this structuring basis as a necessary element to humanize the educational processes and its political, artistic and economic dimensions. It also allows us to conceive humans in their anthropological and sociocultural complexity, and deconstruct the biologizing conception in progress in universal history to safeguard and dignify human existence.

Our parents have an important role in these processes. Through patterns of interaction and a system of knowledge, faith and practices they guide us in creating essential situations to our citizen formation. These processes incorporate new forms and patterns of subjectivity and behavior in our personalities, committed to dignifying human goals, at least in the praxis of my family.

To babble, smile, crawl, play, walk, study, pray, respect, tolerate, commiserate, share, work, love, preserve, undertake and to innovate are verbs that guide my daily practices during the different stages of my physical and spiritual development – actions that are radiated from the family, supporting it. They also move its concepts of the world, and its singular and universal commitments. Nature and culture, forms, contents, development, citizenship, ethics and sustainability are also elements present in this framework that welds the family base and pose new collective responsibilities to build everyone's future.

In my relationships with my family I have abolished lust, gluttony, greed, anger, arrogance, vanity and laziness. I make efforts so that people and institutions don't privatise the world or transform it into a large market. I make tolerance, fraternity and solidarity my main attributes and I combat the use of drugs, environmental pollution, transgenicity that violates human morality, worsening of social inequality and the restriction of freedom. I am not complicit with bioethical violations and the builders of wars. I use our family love as an instrument of peaceful and solidary coexistence, and I use sensitivity, intuition and abstraction to move my responsibility towards the construction of everyone's future. I use human attributes to build sustainable actions with human identities and commitments. Located sustainabilities and committed to people, families, communities, cities, countries, continents, the planet and also with the cosmos. Sustainabilities centered on the short time of the people's physical, psychic and religious needs and, at the same time, responsible for the long time of adaptability and sociability in succession and preservation of the generations and the mankind.

My generation will promote sustainable development. We shall eliminate wars and terrorism, invent non-polluting energy sources, reorganize the land transport sector, replace the current industrial matrix, protect marine natural resources, and qualify the use of soils and the atmosphere. We will concentrate efforts to institutionalize pollution control mechanisms, improve the management of climate change impacts, protect water resources, and preserve biodiversity and natural heritage. We will also develop mechanisms that minimise risks and protect human health in unhealthy occupational matrices, and manage with determination the use of ecotoxicology and the impacts of fungicides and pesticides. Special attention will be given to the mobilization of theoretical and empirical structures of the economic and social sciences for a development centered on human valorization, and in the promotion of literature, arts and culture. Grandpa, my generation will also prioritize the formation of a new civilizing conception committed to the promotion of international cooperation for the elimination of human misery.

These problems are all part of the civilizing legacy of previous generations. We must solve them to build sustainable development during the following centuries. Its solutions require measuring the relational effects between economic and environmental activities, and creating languages that better represent the impacts of ecological risks on societies. We are also inventing mechanisms to solve the problems of social inequality and the distribution of wealth to different societies in the face of difficulty in accessing critical natural resources sources. It will be necessary to build a human language that applies the notion of sustainability in a region or a given territory by promoting diversity and cultures, and developing strategies to integrate ecology into economics and institutional policies, among other factors.

In this century, we will prioritize the fight against poverty and the deterioration of the world's biodiversity, which are worsening at an increasing rate. We will build alternatives to the inappropriate use of soil, water and atmospheres; to the commercial overexploitation of some animal and plant species, and to the introduction of predatory species in certain ecosystems. We will eliminate agriculture with predatory techniques, and we combat predatory rearrangement of territories and global climate change. We will also implement methods and public policies to plan and control accelerated demographic growth, policies of economic development not adapted and not integrated with local and regional environmental realities, and the right of access to natural resources. Everyone will be called to participate in the implementation of new forms of economic development and human coexistence, giving new meaning to humans and societies.

Our concerns and commitments are centered on the process of creating a kind of sustainable development involving people, families, societies and mankind – challenges that bring new elements to the understanding of issues that relate sustainability and education. To what extent does sustainability clarify and determine the degree of importance of education in our social life? How do these forms of education contribute to the organization and development of a sustainable society, focused on cultures and different forms of relationships and lives of peoples? These anxieties are materialized in a type of spiritual commitment, of existential sensitivity committed to the origin and destiny of mankind, in all its dimensions. In 2100, they will unfold in an ecologically preserved world, with less economic inequality and more social inclusion. In a world that will have Amazonia as its main reference and locus of sustainability. Grandpa, I want to see Amazonia.

8. I want to get to know Amazonia

My grandfather taught me that life reveals itself as a process. It does not exist in a certain independente quantity that we can characterize. Life generates life from its basic cellular unit, from our peaceful and fraternal relationship with people, with the environment and mainly through love. Biology finds that the cell is the smallest organic element that has the properties of the living being, the reproduction is made by fertilization, that is, the fusion of two sex cells, sperm and egg. The healthy development of the embryo is made from the egg from the moment it is formed, by the multiplication of cells and its differentiation in specialized cells, in a context moved by love.

In the middle of the 20st century, the birth of molecular biology resulted in a new way of considering living beings. The idea is that the physical and chemical characteristics and properties of living beings must necessarily be explained by the structures and interactions of the molecules that compose them, just as social cohesion is explained by the multiple interactions between individuals, groups, communities and societies.

Grandpa also says that from this assumption, the way of approaching and considering the living being's biological and social studies, its functioning, evolution and its social relations has changed. The demands for molecular and social explanations have been incorporated into the various branches of biology and social sciences. In particular cellular biology, virology, immunology, physiology, neurology, endocrinology, sociology, anthropology, ethics, economics, philosophy and politics resulting in impacts across all sectors of modern science and across a broad technological segment. These assumptions, together with the deciphering of the genetic code, following the discovery of DNA by Watson and Crick in 1953, are fundamental problems of the natural and the social sciences. They made possible the unveiling of heredity and the emergence of transgenics. They also introduced new relationships and historical meanings between the forms of governing in the world, construction and organization of knowledge, productive processes and our religious beliefs.

My grandfather emphasizes that humans are not a physical, chemical and biological machine. To explain their ideas and relationships it is necessary to research their origins in society, not in biology. He affirms that the march of history is determined by social forces, ideas of social origin, and that the history of mankind is more fruitful and complex than the history of matter. Grandpa points out that, at the end of the last century, a new and relevant element was incorporated in this historical process: the concept of sustainability. The possibility of extinction of the human species because of the planet's ecological destabilization has contributed to its emergence and materialization. Continuing, my Grandpa clarifies that this situation reaffirmed the Amazonia's geographical and historical importance to Brazil and the world.

On a large map on the table, Grandpa travels over Brazilian Amazonia, showing me its villages, isolated communities and cities distributed across its 5 million km² territory, home to about 30 million inhabitants. Grandfather explains that the creation of the Earth began with Amazonia. On one of his travels throughout the universe, God stopped on Earth to rest. Worried about the history of the universe, he created time and life cycles. As it was very cold and dark, he caused a small inclination in the Earth's axis of rotation to better illuminate and warm the places later called the tropics. With one breath he spread more than 2,000 rivers in this region, most of them crossing its 11,248 km of borders with Peru, Bolivia, Colombia, Venezuela, Suriname, Guyana and French Guiana, ending in a great river, the largest in the world.

Then, with a flute, God modelled and materialized a man and a woman and – in a quick baptism in the waters of the great river – gave them life. After creating the flora and fauna of this region with synchronized movements of his magic wand, and before continuing his journey, God told the couple: this is your home. You use that canoe to get to know it and guide and clarify your descendants about its importance to them and mankind's future. The man called the woman "Ama" and the woman called him "Izona;" they called the great Amazon river, and its great home, Amazonia. For thousands of years, with their descendants, they cared for the region, built their cultural forests and made their inventory to better protect it from the greed of adventurers.

My grandfather invited me to see 3.9 million km^2 of its forests, explaining to me about the rich biological diversity of its flora and fauna, and the cycles of nature that produce and move life in the region.

He insists on presenting to me its inventory that registers 517 species of amphibians (71% of Brazil and 10% of the world) that, during their cycles of aquatic and terrestrial life, transport the spirits of the forests in their travels through the forests and rivers; 3,000 species of fish (50% of South and Central America and 23% of the world) that populate its rivers and water streams and fly among the trees to escape the intense catch to which they are subjected; 486 species of reptiles (81% of Brazil and 6% of the world) that form a large army of alligators, turtles, snakes and lizards essential to its ecological stability; 16,000 species of superior plants (93% of Brazil and 17% of the world) that sow smells, corners and lives in all directions, renewing our air and producing and reproducing life in the forests, transforming solar energy into organic matter that feeds and moves its cycles; 427 species of mammals (81% of Brazil and 9% of the world) that suckle the beings of the forest protecting them from tropical diseases and human arrogance; and 1,622 species of birds (77% from Brazil and 13% from the world) that sow and recreate its natural gardens and constitute its eyes and radars, monitoring its territories and making its regional and worldwide communication.

Grandpa explains to me that although the laws of botany, entomology, zoology, physics and chemistry are intertwined, they cannot explain the beauty of life in the region. It is illuminated and sustained by a complex cultural and physical system which is continually renewed, and overflowing to other regions of the planet.

Culture, energy, organic matter, water and the spirits of the forests and the rivers rule life in Amazonia. It is home to 163 different indigenous cultures and it is irrigated by the Amazon river that drains more than 7 million hectares of its lands, leading to the Atlantic Ocean 176 million liters of water per second (176,000 m^3/s). This water flow exceeds the Congo river in Africa (the second in volume of water) four times and the Mississippi river ten times. Amazonia is home to the largest surface fresh water source on the planet. Grandfather declares that the Amazonas river's average water flow in a second is sufficient for the daily supply of a city with 294,000 inhabitants. He also says that the Amazonian basin is an inhabited region with one of the largest rainfall indices on the planet. It has an average precipitation of 2,200 mm/year (1 mm of precipitation corresponds to one litre of water per square metre). This represents the volume of 12,000 trillion liters (12 × 10^{12} m^3) of water in liquid form, which this region receives each year. This results in the largest hydrographic basin in the world and in a mythical universe inhabited by the snakes, mermaids and enchanted porpoises.

My grandfather insists on the existence of a sea of water below and another above the Amazonia, making it always wet and illuminated. He relates that this peculiar characteristic of the region has a strong relationship with its forms of life and with the solar energy it receives. Therefore, my grandfather says that there are the "flying rivers" in the Amazonian atmosphere, a complex hydrographical basin on its solid surface, and large hydrological reservoirs in its subsoil, not yet properly dimensioned. Understanding nature's engineering operation here presents a great challenge for future generations.

Grandfather explains that the Amazonian and Congo basins and the area around Borneo are typically tropical. They are important to Earth's ecological stability and efficient in the absorption of solar energy and its redistribution via atmosphere (Crutzen and Andrae, 1990). Recent studies project that the humidity conversion process (through rainfall) in Amazonia's atmosphere liberates heat equivalent to approximately 400 million megawatts. This energy is essential to Amazonia's maintenance and to the thermodynamic stability of global atmospheric processes. Energy radiated by Amazonia, warming the relations between peoples and enhancing the full splendor of the germination of vegetable life in the agricultural areas and social life in the cities and the fields.

Grandpa also points out that pollution from industrial and automobile matrices is poisoning the atmosphere and the courses of water. He clarifies the importance of participation of the Amazonian ecosystems in the basic processes indispensable to chemical stability of the terrestrial atmosphere. Amazonia contributes to the control of the main greenhouse gases, in particular, carbon dioxide, nitrous oxide, nitric oxide and nitrogen dioxide. The participation of the first two gases in climate stability of the atmosphere and the other two in chemical stability, on a planetary scale, constitute complex problems related to the possibility of the planet's ecological destabilization.

According to Grandpa, burning the forest releases many contaminants into the atmosphere, hazardous to the population's health. Children are most affected by this type of pollution. Together, the four countries with the highest carbon dioxide emissions in 2014, at a total of about 62% of global carbon dioxide emissions, were China (30%), the United States of America (15%), the European Union (10%), and India (7%). This is worrying. Grandpa also explains that, in 2018, 37 billion tons of carbon dioxide were effectively emitted into the Earth's atmosphere, and that the Amazonian forests behave like "giant air vacuum cleaners," absorbing up to 500 million tons annually (15.85 tons per second) of this carbon dioxide, for photosynthetic synthesis. Carbon is the main food of the forests, being essential for it to produce wood and leaves, and to renew its plant and animal life.

Amazonia is a key region in this worldwide process. Current lack of control over the growth of deforestation and burning in this region is a worldwide concern. Mankind's future is also intertwined with the preservation of Amazonia.

My grandfather warns that deforestation hinders the process of regeneration of life and intensifies the warming of the planet. He also explains that the Amazonian biomes store 100 billion tons of carbon, 10% of the total carbon existing in the Earth's atmosphere.

Sitting under a chestnut tree, Grandfather states to me that Brazilian Amazonia represents 3/5 of Brazil's territory; 3/5 of Pan-American Amazonia; 2/5 of South America; 1/20 of its terrestrial surface; 3/1000 of the world population; 1/5 of the world availability of surface fresh water; 50% of Brazil's hydroelectric potential; around 1/3 of the planet's rainforests; 1/3 of the world's biodiversity; 12 million hectares of floodplains; 75,000 km of navigable rivers; 1/10 of the universal biota; 163 indigenous peoples corresponding to 384 thousand people (38% of Brazilian indigenous peoples); 250 languages spoken in its Pan-American extension, of which 140 in the Brazilian part.

It is fantastic! The region has more than 2,000 rivers. Experts have already identified more than 11,676 tree species in Amazonia, distributed over 1,225 genera and 140 families. Amazonia is strategic to the development of bioindustry. Studies estimate the existence of 16,000 species of trees in the region. Certainly, this great living library has answers to many of mankind's problems. Amazonia is home to 19% of the world's tree species. It is home to the world's largest genetic bank on solid land or the largest botanical garden on the planet. Its connections with economic processes are important for mankind's future.

Grandpa cites as an example the discoveries of chloroquine and hydroxychloroquine that are synthetic drugs manufactured through modelling referenced on a natural molecule found in the quina tree, a species of Amazonian rainforest. Today this medication is being researched as a complementary use to combat covid-19. For a long time, the bark of quina has been used by indigenous peoples from Amazonia to cure their patients. During the 18st century it was taken to Europe by the Jesuits and widely used in the treatment of malaria. In the 20st century, the quinine, the bioactive molecule of quina, was industrialized by the pharmaceutical industry and its widespread use in medical prescriptions. I tell

Grandpa that, really, Amazonia is a large living library waiting for its books to be deciphered for the benefit of mankind. A marvel for the bioindustry. Brazilian leaders should prioritize the financing of science and technology projects in the region, aimed at the manufacture of new products.

With great emotion, Grandpa clarifies to me that the intense process of evaporation of the Amazonian trees creates a 'flying river' above this great tropical forest, which moves according to the planetary atmospheric currents. Grandpa also states that recently a colleague of his, through geological studies, discovered another great river, 4,000 meters below the Amazon river's trough. This new river, named 'Hamza', runs for 6,000 km in Amazonia until it flows into the Atlantic Ocean. Grandpa says that this Amazonian phenomenon is another great blessing from the gods: three great rivers that simultaneously communicate between themselves, with the Amazonian cultures and environments and with the world. Then, Grandpa states that the ecological and cultural destruction of Amazonia will certainly accelerate the emergence of new pandemics and suffering to its peoples and to mankind.

Grandfather, Amazonia is Brazilian people's great patrimony, a challenge for our and the next generations of Brazil. We don't have to be afraid of our future; it necessarily crosses Amazonia. Its humanization and sacred protection, celestial protection, ecological preservation, annunciation, and revelation for sustainable use, for the benefit of Brazilians and mankind, are reasons of satisfaction for everyone.

Grandpa comments that Amazonia's economic potential increases as its importance to the planetary ecological stability is reaffirmed, creating new forms of political and social relations in the region. He emphasizes the insistence of politicians and NGOs to redistribute and slice it into fiefdoms with the creation of new states, territories and numerous reserves and forest units under its control. It also talks about Brazil's political inability to propose an integrated development model for the region, and clarifies that its economic matrix is still the same one planned and implemented 50 years ago, unrelated to its cultural and geographical characteristics, although this picture is in a slow process of change.

In this dialogue with Grandpa, I identified the main issues that Amazonia poses to the world. Its sustainable development in condition of largest living library on the planet. Its existence as global ecological and symbolic processes, and its physical presence as strategic spaces for Brazil and the world. Its relevance as a thermostat and ecological recycling source for the planet, and its socioeconomic and cultural importance for Brazil. Finally, its important role as a mechanism of the planet's climate stability.

I keep interrupting Grandpa, who is already tired, telling him that I am impressed by the beauty, the peculiarities and the secrets hidden in Amazonia. I tell him that I have concluded that Amazonia plays similar roles to a large machine to produce heat and redistribute it towards the planet, and as a gigantic vacuum cleaner that cleans the Earth's atmosphere. It also functions as an enormous refrigerator cooling the planet, and a large recycling machine that returns to nature physical, chemical and biological waste in new forms beneficial to the development of life on the planet.

I also deduced that Amazonia is a historical construction of its peoples, of their relations with its environments and of their intercultural relations. Its myths and rites, matrices of animal and vegetable lives, the geometric shapes and the flavors from its forest, the sweet, the bitter and other combinations; some structures of thought and typologies of white man's colonialist imaginary that only the inhabitants of the waters and forests know how to decipher; its diversity of sociologies and anthropologies; its poetry and its songs of the trees, birds, fish and animals are cultural legacies that move the world concepts of its 163 peoples. People who know the sounds and silences of the forest, and the spirits of everything that exists in nature, because they are creators and creations. They are the ones who understand the existence and movements of the Moon, the Sun and the stars in the firmament, that have always accompanied them during their spiritual evolution, and their struggles against the greed of predatory capitalism to protect their cultures and territories.

Grandpa, grandmother told me that you published a book on Amazonia by Peter Lang Publishing. Why did you publish this book? To present and disseminate Amazonia's world importance, and denounce its full openness to the actions of predatory productive forces by the Brazilian ruler. This book warns people, societies and world governments about the tendency of irreversible destruction of Amazonia, promoted by the Brazilian president's actions in this region since 2020.

In this book called "The Future of Amazonia in Brazil; A Worldwide Tragedy," together with your grandmother, we have analyzed structuring issues of this region: Why is Amazonia the last ecocultural utopia of mankind? What problems does it pose to the world and why is it important to mankind? What are the relationships between science, religion, Amazonia and sustainability? Why does predatory capitalism have no theoretical or empirical scope to transform Amazonia into a sustainable environmental commodity? How can we protect it from human stupidity and market greed? Why has the Brazilian ruler become a weapon against Amazonia? How can it be developed in a sustainable way for the benefit of the Brazilian people and mankind?

I tell you that Amazonia's future remains very uncertain. The decrease in international political pressure and the total demobilization of environmental inspection during the covid-19 pandemic have contributed to the increasing deforestation in the region.

In contrast, the Brazilian president's incentive to the possession and illegal use of indigenous lands by prospectors and loggers, and his threat to revise consolidated indigenous rights are another perverse legacy resulting from Jair Bolsonaro. The growing expansion of agribusiness in Amazonia and the recent authorization by the Brazilian president of 51 different types of highly toxic pesticides are also threats to its indigenous peoples. Agribusiness continues to advance through Amazonia, creating poverty for its populations, deforesting and contaminating its biomes. Grandpa reaffirms that the Brazilian ruler continues to deny protecting Brazilian Amazonia's 163 indigenous peoples. According to Grandpa, there is an ethnocide of indigenous cultures in Amazonia that has intensified with covid-19 propagated by the invaders of their lands. The Brazilian ruler has not only been silent but has

63

helped covid-19 spread in the indigenous lands in Amazonia. From May 2021, more than 20,000 cases of contamination and 1,000 deaths of indigenous peoples by covid-19 were recorded in Amazonia – a tragedy that keeps growing. I was shocked by Grandpa's words, but very challenged by the great problems that Amazonia poses for my generation.

I continued my journey around the world, impressed and challenged by the responsibilities of Brazil and international organizations to develop this heritage and treasure that is Amazonia. But very happy to know the importance of the Amazonian peoples in the process of its construction and preservation, reaffirming the need to conceive and implement models of development that don't destroy nature and are not based on amorality, on money, on morbid rationalism or on autistic attitudes. After seeing Amazonia, my life changed radically, for the better. All of the world's young people should get to know Amazonia. Thanks Grandpa, I love you so much. I was impressed by the beauty and grandeur of the Amazon river – transporting life, joy and history to the whole world. The Amazon river commands sustainability in Amazonia. Its waters bless us all. Grandpa, I am thrilled but I must continue my journey. Please publish this short poem I made in honor of the largest river in the world.

9. Amazon river; life and joy

Amazon river; life and joy

Amazon river
Ever onward
A light for us all

Bringing joy and life

Amazon river, let our love
Protect Amazonia

Amazon river
Spread our cultures around the world
Make our hearts and minds fruitful
Let our fauna, flora and birds live free

Amazon river
Put an end to the evils in the world
Irrigate soils and crops
Quench our thirst and bathe our sorrows

Amazon river
Don't give up on us
Tell the sea that no one owns this planet
Protect our forests and our indigenous peoples

Amazon river, let our love
Protect Amazonia

Amazon river, for love of your children
Cool the environments of our world
Shine light on our future
Bless us all

Au revoir l'Amazonie, notre amour
Goodbye Amazonia, our love
Amazon, let our love
Protect Amazonia
Victim of covid-19

Grandpa, this poem illustrates my understanding of the relationship between Amazonia and sustainability.

10. My contribution to sustainability

I listened attentively to Grandpa speaking about covid-19, mankin's future and Amazonia. Grandfather has emphasized the collective fear that people have of this wave of pain, suffering and uncontrolled death because of the pandemic. Grandfather identifies the traumas and reaffirms the necessary response of mankind after this world tragedy, showing that it is necessary to create the future from our current realities. He clarifies Amazonia's importance at this juncture that embraces all peoples and different global social and economic interests. I have concluded that sustainability permeates all these issues and it is a key element in improving public policies and societies. When grandfather introduced me to Amazonia, I said little and offered fragmented and provisional words. I immediately learned that the relationship between Amazonia and sustainable development is very clear. Sustainability is inextricably intertwined with the processes that move life and the relationships between human beings, nature and their peers.

From this foundation, I concluded that there are not only two types of sustainability – that of poor countries and the other of rich countries, or that of rich people and the other for poor people. Therefore, sustainability cannot be isolated from the symbolic and subjective representations of human nature.

Sustainability and happiness, sustainability and solidarity, sustainability and fraternity, sustainability and peace, sustainability and social inclusion, sustainability and the arts, sustainability and religions are fundamental predicates for its historical legitimation. Sustainability is not a product that can be made available on supermarket shelves. It is a new attribute for people's citizenship, similar to the representations of love, happiness, peace, solidarity, tolerance, freedom, and also pleasure. Sustainability, contrary to what is expressed in scientific literature, represents attributes of reason and also of the heart.

It is a universal "good" accessible to all peoples and an instrument committed to combating socioeconomic inequalities and to social inclusions, everywhere and at all times. It is not only a solution, but also a method that will guide the reflection and justification of choices. Our mothers, teachers, friends and communities must make a pact with sustainability: to consider it a new "food" of life.

Listening to people, I deduce that in general public managers have an evolutionary, reductionist and mechanistic conception of human beings and nature. To economists, engineers and most professionals in the natural sciences, natural environments are made up of trees, rivers, birds, animals and microorganisms guided by the laws of physics, chemistry and biology. These gentlemen, for example, consider that trees are mechanisms for accumulation of carbon and nitrogen, in greater proportion, to be submitted to the processes of surplus-value. They ignore that, to the traditional populations, such as those of Amazonia, America, Africa, Asia and Australia, the forests are cultural constructions that incorporate their spirits. They are part of their mythological representations, which, in turn, are fused into their existence. For these peoples, the forest is not only matter – it communicates with their ponderable and imponderable worlds. For them, the forest is not a commodity, it is priceless.

Grandfather told me that, when he was a child, he received a tree as a gift from his father. At every move of the household, the tree went with him. Almost whispering, Grandpa also told me that Grandma was very jealous of his friendship with the big and leafy tree that he called "Hope." Grandpa commented that one day, when he woke up, he realized that "Hope" had disappeared, and had gone away without leaving any trace. "Hope" never returned, leaving Grandpa desolate, but resigned because he still believes that it is now in a heavenly plane.

The ideas prevailing in the press, media and political discourses are impregnated with excluding assumptions, scientific and economic approaches and practices. The dynamics of these scientific and economic processes are based on a principle that sees nature as independent of humans. This contributed to crystallizing a Western conception in which the 'human condition' is subject and subverted to the processes of biologization or naturalization of nature.

Science denies the indivisibility between nature and culture, contributing to the prevalence of universal thought with a privatist and functional character; the term indivisibility has the connotation of reciprocal existence, of an intrinsic existential fusion intertwined to these two entities, humans and nature.

But Grandpa, is not the oxygen I breathe vital to my survival? Isn't 60% of my body made up of water? Every day, when I go to sleep, don't I pray? Grandpa, it is very easy to understand that I don't exist separately from nature and the universe with everything within it, including my family, friends and religion.

Another contradiction present in this exclusionary social process refers to the 'cultural strangeness' that has racism as its main manifestation, a problem not yet solved in the contemporary world. Grandpa, why is human being racist? There are no races. Our origin is common. Racism has been built by militarist and slave imperialism since the colonial period. And certainly, the first sapiens human appeared in Africa or Asia. Grandpa, how African and Asian people are beautiful, cheerful and intelligent.

These two foundations, the 'cultural strangeness' and the confrontation 'nature×culture' were the main agents of the process of formation of European culture. They played an important role in the matrices of the models of social and economic development, which have been radiated throughout the planet. They contributed to the fact that politics, economics and science put themselves at the service of non-sustainability, local and global, at all scales. In general, political and economic analyses are very superficial. They ignore the richness of human subjectivity, the diversity of choices and desires, the moral and affective, aesthetic and social dimensions of mankind.

Grandfather, as I already mentioned, mankind has a great cultural diversity. This is the main foundation of sustainability. Reaffirming alterity, protecting the socially excluded and creating a new multicultural world are commitments that I make on behalf of my generation.

From a human perspective, sustainability must be associated with a public initiative that is committed to implementing a food security policy that privileges the most socially fragile communities. Food is not a commodity; it is a social good that must be within the economic reach of all who are hungry. Global sustainability requires eliminating hunger and greater public control of agricultural areas and the food trade. It demands instituting the ethical and human commitment to insert people in the market to meet their needs. In the sustainability's world there are no abandoned and hungry children.

Grandpa, my generation is receiving a very depreciated world. The intensified destruction of natural environments requires creating a political pact that integrates conservation and land use actions, involving people, communities, organizations, national institutions, parliaments, national and international forums, multilateral institutions and, depending on the scales of these actions, the world public opinion. It is necessary to develop strategies that combine nature's use and conservation, exploitation and replacement of stocks, ecologically correct production and commercialization, private enterprise and cooperativism, and convergence technologies and technological development. Highlight also for environmental education and citizenship, and circular economy and sustainable development.

Grandfather, I also note that there are numerous characteristics of sustainability that have its own identities, which makes it difficult to construct a standard methodology that is applied in a generalized manner to different cultures and socio-environmental realities. Interregional and national social and economic inequalities contribute to these difficulties.

In my travels around the world, I witness the social precarization of most communities, with a high degree of illiteracy, unemployment and lack of basic policies. I also saw the collapse of land use in large concentrations of private lands that are being poisoned by economic groups, the demobilisation and social disorganisation in most countries, and the lack of mechanisms to share traditional wisdom with scientific and technological knowledge. The absence of infrastructure, at all levels, making it impossible to create productive chains based on technological inventions and, at the same time, to incorporate the appropriate technologies, specific to the different places and regions, has contributed to the collapse of various public policies.

I also note the lack of technical conditions that make the products of isolated communities competitive, has contributed to their remaining enslaved and hostages to speculators. Similarly, the absence of policies of sustainable credit and appropriate to different regional realities, and the need to create the economic and environmental zoning of strategic regions are challenges for public managers. This situation is essential to the establishment and integration of community productive actions.

It is imperative that these mechanisms incrust sustainable practices in a juncture of generosity and collective commitments that dignify people and their practices. Creating a more cheerful world is another important dimension of sustainability. Grandpa, covid-19 has aggravated this perverse situation.

I have also observed that religions, beliefs and traditions of people and societies have a strong influence on their relationships with nature. This human dimension needs to be better understood for the correct establishment of the operational mechanisms of sustainability. In general, the human-nature relationship is typified as anthropocentric or non-anthropocentric. The first conception considers the world spinning around human beings with its full dominion over the processes of use and commodification of nature. This conception considers nature isolated from the human condition. It has originated an environmental ethic that creates norms and guidelines to guide the market and people on the best forms of relationships with nature. But always from the perspective of economic processes. The non-anthropocentric conception is based on the process of encrusting the human condition in nature, forming an inseparable whole. This conception is prevalent in several eastern cultures and world mythologies, to different degrees.

Grandpa, the discussion about the prevalence of the global impacts because one or other of these tendencies is sterile and unproductive. Both tendencies are legitimized by its respective political systems as well as by the science and technology that, in general, have methodologies and protocols standardized on a global scale.

Another example that reinforces this argument is based on the accelerated depreciation of natural environments around the planet, including Eastern ones. Urban and rural pollution in India and China are unique examples. In general, non-anthropocentrism in the human-nature relationship in the East has a growing disconnection with its educational and industrial practices. A quick local survey or analysis of specialized literature and its platforms of productive arrangements proves this assertion. The political discourses of public authorities, west and east, completely diverge from the environmental and health realities in their respective countries. This false binary logic, anthropocentrism versus non-anthropocentrism, needs to be deconstructed with new forms of human-nature relationships. Grandpa, this initiative is fundamental to the success of sustainability.

Global's new challenges require to construct convivial forms and productive arrangements that protect the people, mankind and the planet at all scales. Sustainability places new elements into this process of worldwide interest, now and in the future, and here and in the world. Sustainability needs to be based on cultures, but not necessarily on the immobilizing traditions and current forms of organization of industrialized societies with their environments.

Grandpa, I propose a material and symbolic structure in the form of layers for sustainability. This structure will allow multiple and simultaneous human interactions between people and their local and global environments. Cultures and technologies will lead this process based on convergence technologies. Grandpa, today, the people are here and there, simultaneously. Our policies on food, health, education, housing, mobility, production, among others, must be radically modified. They have to consider the body but also the human spirit imbricated to nature.

The operationalization of this proposal requires establishing a network of international cooperation centers in the planet's strategic places, and the transformation of various natural environments into world heritage. These centers will have a strategic role to strengthen basic public policies, collaborating to integrate the impoverished local and regions in sustainable development programs from a global perspective. In this new configuration the site local be interwoven to the global, on sustainable technical bases. Grandpa, the world is already fully radiographed and monitored by GPS and other spatial and temporal coordinate platforms. These electronic systems can be used in real time to subsidize the construction of these local-world technical structures aimed at regional, national and world sustainability.

Grandpa, the covid-19 pandemic's case is paradigmatic. From Wuhan, a city in Central China, this virus quickly spread around the world, exterminating hundreds of thousands of lives. There are strong indications that this devastating virus is due to imbalance between humans' relationships with nature, especially with animals and wild birds. There are also technical opinions that attribute the creation of this virus to scientific laboratories. This case has not been confirmed. Grandfather, the history of mankind is asymmetrical. It is impossible to reverse the movement of a historical event. Time does not go back. A pandemic that spreads toward the world from one place cannot return to this same place keeping everything preserved as before. This is also true for climate change, which raises many concerns for us all due to its known deleterious impacts as well as those still unknown. Grandpa, time measured on clocks will not be the main chronological reference for my generation. I will invent another type of time. The time of sustainability. It will be a measure of generosity and social promotion.

Leaders and economists find it very difficult to prioritize and solve the world's economic problems. They are slaves to the market. Most of them act as if they were lobotomized, without sensitivity and soul. Many of them are trained to use human knowledge, a 'common good' of mankind, in the form of merchandise to oppress and exploit society's great segments. Our future cannot be held hostage by politics and the economy, which must have better control of organised societies.

Grandfather, I have no difficulty in dialoguing with friendly children from Africa, Japan, the United States, France, Australia and other countries. We talk about everything; our families, schools, favorite entertainment, cities, physical beauties of our countries, and our sustainable future. Through WhatsApp, Skype and other electronic devices we transport ourselves to joint meetings where we express desires and proposals to make our planet healthier and happier. Young people's proposals to improve people's lives and the planet are never considered by adults, and also by public authorities. Families and educational systems have oppressed and treated the young as the future labor of the market. Grandfather, the world demands radical changes. We are active actors in this process of change that requires new approaches, attitudes and responsibilities. Today, we are privatized according to the interests of economic groups. Young people have no life plans, and growing unemployment is their greatest enemy. We will accelerate the change in this social and economic framework.

My beloved grandson, in the physical sciences the concept of work is related to physical forces in motion. They are these forces that generate new forms and content to the properties of matter. They are responsible for the beauty of nature. The meaning of the concept of work in the economic sciences needs to change. It cannot be used to exploit the worker and as a pretext for the accumulation of wealth. He should promote human beings and generate happiness.

For my generation, the problems presented in this dialogue between us are not impediments to the emergence of sustainability. On the contrary, it is necessary to center it on cultures, articulating it with social inclusion, entrepreneurship and innovation in collective and long-range structures. It is also necessary to enhance the socioeconomic conditions of places, regions and countries from a perspective of local sustainable development. In this broader context, I notice that the 'role' of sustainability in the world is different from the 'role' of the world in sustainability.

Grandson, it is important that you understand the questions that I will present next. I have noticed that the notion of sustainable development still has structural problems, among which there are six major issues. All of them relate to the forms of organisation of economies and societies.

The first is symbolic, and therefore the most complex. There is a certain illusion about the notion of sustainability, which considers that the mechanisms that make it operational don't establish "where, when, and how" to replace the classical form of development. It is possible that the wait will be for something that will never happen; we run the risk of constructing a socio-economic enterprise that is so unsound that it will never materialize.

Secondly, there is incompatibility between the notion of sustainability and the concept of growth – not financial growth, rather the growth of the flow of mass and energy. This will result in prioritizing the marketing of goods with greater durability and changing the world's industrial matrix, implementing clean development mechanisms.

The third problem concerns the dynamics surrounding the process of financial accumulation. Core countries are becoming richer and the peripheral countries are becoming poorer. This situation demands the incorporation of the notion of sustainability, including those essential requirements for a basic standard of living. There is also an additional problem: the increasing global wave of privatization of the world conspires against the management of the planet's natural wealth.

Fourth, hypocrisy exists within central country governments. History has recorded the discourse of leaders that oppose practical action. They will not act in any way that might risk the welfare of their voters and their economic and political stability.

Fifth, the notion of sustainable development has historical validity only in local experiments. Yet, there is a common objective: the preservation of biodiversity associated with cultural diversity. The objective conditions for preservation remain controversial. Disregard for the biosphere and the standard capitalist approach to exploiting natural resources obstruct attempts to find solutions.

Finally, there is an increasing tension between the notion of sustainability and the universal principle of national security. The friction generated will depend on the evolution of political processes on a worldwide scale. Grandpa, the great global economic recession due to covid-19 has added new difficulties in this framework.

I note that fragments of these six issues that drive the notion of sustainability in global processes are present in various regional and national development models, with impacts on its basic public policies.

On one hand, the construction of the structural conditions to consolidate sustainable development on a global scale has an economic and political cost that leaders of industrialized countries have not yet taken on. On the other hand, the social actors have developed strategies to incorporate the 'human condition' as the main assumption of sustainability. This perspective is a challenge for the education, science and technology policies in the 21st century.

Incorporate these assumptions, in a humanistic way, to the behavioral and cognitive patterns of children's personality formation, creating multiple convergences between theoretical knowledge, praxis, fictional imaginary and sustainable practices will result in a more fruitful and generous future for all. Grandpa, today the world situation is more complex. It requires more dialogue and solidarity between leaders that are focused on fighting covid-19.

So, grandson, the cartography of sustainability shows that its role in the world is based on the diverse compositions of its forms and contents. All committed to the perennials of the human species and the planet, through public policies. It also shows that the world's role in sustainability is linked to the collapse of the models of standard development. This requires the re-signification of the concepts of economic development and citizenship. This also requires a mankind more committed to its future and worried about social issues.

I notice that these two 'roles' are seated on mobile and non-coincident structures and enterprises, most of the time with a strong dependence on political, economic, scientific, religious and media processes, on a global scale. This new political centrality requires the emergence of sustainability from the located enterprises. A process guided by a temporal metric that articulates the brief time of social needs to the long time of the generations and the preservation of the planet. It is an important foundation of our civilizing process and the future of my generation. The contradictions that move this framework must be solved by the next generations. Global policy management needs collective governance. A policy management, simultaneously, shared and centralized, and moved by the regionalized powers.

This new framework will require the deployment of a new global system of tributary and fiscal control. The creation of a new global currency and the establishment of new forms of production and circulation of goods will be crucial for the economic and social success of this new initiative. The creation of a new global currency will be decisive for the economic and social success of this new initiative.

My contribution to sustainability presents new commitments to education, science and technology, critical media and communication. The processes of organization and functioning of the market and the work matrices will also undergo radical changes. However, the incorporation of ecology to the civilizing process has changed the traditional public policies and the societies' forms of organization. Operational aspects of global sustainability through normative and legal regulations integrated to cultures and unequal socioeconomic sectors are feasible and necessary enterprises. This juncture also challenges religions, organised societies and the global financial market. Grandpa, I have understood what you have said and will present my concerns and appreciations using various examples I have selected in my readings.

Levelling sustainability by abundance rather than scarcity is an attribute that we have to exercise systematically. The dynamics of sustainable development depends on solving complex problems. For example, I note that the impact of pollution on our lives, in a broad way, involves not only financial issues, but also includes value judgments, an eminently political characteristic. There is still difficulty in measuring the effects of gas pollution on our health. However it is already known that the precipitation of acid rains and the formation of ozone from the break of molecules of nitrogen oxides by ultraviolet radiation accelerate the evolution of several chronic diseases, such as asthma, for example.

It is controversial to state that pollution is the only responsible for the death of a person, however, this factor can accelerate it. What are the emotional and financial costs of decreasing life expectancy, immobilisation processes, hospitalisations, collateral effects of medication and loss of a person's youth due to the action of a particular pollutant?

Another symptomatic example refers to the impacts of the greenhouse effect associated with the increasing accumulation of carbon dioxide and other greenhouse gases – atmospheric gases that regulate the amount of heat from the sun absorbed by the Earth. Environmental economic models, which already incorporate this dimension into its structures, project only the costs of private property or of the usufruct rights of human beings.

They don't include the risk of extinction of various animal and plant species, the possibilities of irreversible deleterious impacts on agricultural processes, biogeochemical cycles, and heat and water cycles. Impacts on climatology, places, cities, countries, continents and the planet should also be considered. Grandpa recently told me that doubling the concentration of carbon dioxide in the atmosphere will result in a drop in the world economy of between 3% and 4%.

The connections between genetics, biodiversity, climate change (greenhouse effect, El ninho, etc.) and nanotechnology, and this latter with the development of new materials are paradigmatic examples of a new Era of the world economy during the 21st century. This situation strengthens the geopolitical importance of tropical regions and sustainability.

Finally, Grandpa, modern science and technology are unable to stop the accelerated stage of ecological destruction of the planet, not least because these same scientific and technological processes provide this depreciation. Mankind reaffirms the importance of creating new scientific approaches and structures, as well as sustainable models of economic development. This is a political decision that needs to be exercised immediately.

Grandpa comments that the big economic groups are mainly responsible for the destruction of the planet. I tell him that exacerbated misery in underdeveloped countries also accelerates the destruction of the world's major ecosystems, making sustainable practices more difficult. Human misery continues to be considered as if it were a choice and not a relationship, a social construction. Historically, the market and the liberal policies of national leaders reproduce and recreate misery at intensities and speeds that best serve their specific interests. Mistakenly, the supreme power attributed to private property continues to be placed above the values of life.

Grandpa, the rapid spread of covid-19 has freed the world's misery. Presently, the media and NGOs are making a radiography of this misery. It has gained more visibility. It is a depressing and shameful social framework for leaders and mankind. The condition of sustainability when applied to these countries, in general, reinforces the concept of "biologizing" condemning its populations to eternal socioeconomic isolation, with destructive reverberations to their public policies. The economic level of developing countries can improve with the massive and controlled incorporation of scientific knowledge and technology in its public policies, in an integrated form to the traditional knowledge and to the culture of its peoples. This strategy will create demands for goods and services with major impacts on structural unemployment in developed countries, and will enable a rapid and continuous improvement of quality of life of the populations of poor countries with a faster transition to sustainable levels. It will create universal conditions for more qualified economic development.

Grandfather, nature is present in everything we do. There is a strong relationship between ecology and sustainable development. Intense concentration of people in cities, intensive industrialization based on the use of fossil fuels, the planet's exacerbated privatization, and the disorderly occupation of soil and natural environments are factors that contribute to climate change. Other elements also contribute to the planet's ecological destruction, such as: uncontrolled intervention in the cycles of nature, deforestation and burning of large tropical areas, pollution of the planet's waters, soils and atmosphere, and the compulsive consumerism of rich countries' societies. The difficulty in creating a political consensus among industrialized countries aggravates this global crisis. At this juncture, ecology becomes a field of knowledge and strategic action for mankind. Grandpa, in this context, ecology must be understood as a process of production, development and reproduction of life. This framework has accelerated the implementation of a set of political actions of global reach, especially sustainable development. In other words, the economic, political and scientific actors articulate themselves to rescue and hegemonize a universal conception based on the idea of world-environment, whose context is the destiny of mankind according to the Enlightenment thought from the 18st century. A conception that virtually seeks to make humans-nature-culture eternal and invincible.

Grandpa explains that sustainable development, in the limit, tries to construct strategies, methods and mechanisms that make possible to reconcile economic development with ecological stability, in a participatory dimension. It proposes valuing traditional knowledge by integrating it to scientific and technological knowledge in an ethical perspective that radiates from the singular to universal, and local towards the global.

However, these ethics present great problems facing the globalization of technical and scientific culture. Modern science methodologically presumes the distinction between fact and value, and recognizes itself as ethically neutral, remaining in a strictly extrinsic relationship with the sphere of good. And with an additional problem: in the technological field, the operational mechanisms of this notion require the replacement of the current energy matrix as a central priority. They also impose the relativization of the concept of financial accumulation. This concept is the driving force of the process of production, expansion and circulation of capital. This is a necessary tool to create, modulate and make perennial the pillars of development processes, sustained or not.

The notion of sustainability also does not explain the necessary inclusion of the social contract, a legal instrument that gives historicity to development. Despite these many difficulties, according to Grandpa, mankind already has enough wisdom to create collective solutions to these problems.

The construction of a new civilizing genesis based on a process of multicultural humanization, and integrated to the global ethnic and political solidarities constitutes an emblematic reference to interweave ecology in development, and vice versa, creating the technical and political conditions necessary for the emergence of social, economic and environmental sustainability.

Several difficulties are presented for the interruption of the process of pauperization and ecological destruction of the planet. Highlight to the resistance of the transnational economic groups, industrialized countries's lack of political determination, and high financial costs for the implementation of a new non-polluting industrial matrix. The construction of a joint action by hegemonic leaders in the realization of a 'principle of responsibility' that reconciles the ongoing economic interests and the worldwide humanistic commitments is also a major global challenge. The poor socioeconomic configurations in most of the underdeveloped countries aggravate this juncture. The emergence and crystallization of clientelist and authoritarian leaders as well as the absence of democracy, institutionalised corruption, disrespect for human rights, political manipulation, control over the media, spurious agreements and the absence of organised civil society these countries contribute to this situation.

Grandpa, nobody is born with these moral deformities. Our families, schools, social environments and political systems contribute to incorporating these evils in our minds and hearts. This needs to change.

Today it is necessary to create a civilizing concept committed to the preservation of the planet and to the perpetuity of mankind. This genesis requires institutionalizing political conceptions committed to cultural and racial diversity, social differences and inequalities, tolerance and generosity. It is also necessary to plan and implement new educational policies, at all levels, contextualized and integrated to an economic, human and solidarity development. In this context, free and quality public education at all levels must be taken on as a collective achievement and a universal right. For this reason it cannot be subject to market regulation. Grandfather, during the period of the covid-19 pandemic, distance learning has been implemented and regulated in public and private education networks. The construction of new methodologies and evaluation mechanisms for digital education is another challenge for public managers.

Grandpa, in my travels around the world I have lived with mankind's complexities. I realize that since the 1950s, science and technology have played a leading role in world development. They enabled the organization of structures, systems and processes of construction of new products and management programs directed at improving people and societies. They have helped organise and improve the outreach and effectiveness of public policies. They have also made it possible to eradicate diseases, increase life expectancy, reduce poverty and hunger, revolutionize education systems, and to promote radical changes in the transport and communication systems. They have developed robotics and cybernetics, allowed us to explore outer space, popularize arts and cultures, create new war artefacts, globalize the economy and increase the material wealth of nations.

My beloved grandfather, unfortunately, this same science and technology has also been instrumentalized to increase social and economic inequality and destroy the planet's ecological stability. The advancement of technology has not prevented the illness of a large part of the world's societies contaminated by covid-19. People have suffered a lot from the death of family and friends because of covid-19.

Grandson: In general, patients of covid-19 die alone in hospitals, very afraid and terrified to be prevented from saying goodbye to their family and friends. Another issue that frightens people is the verification that this pandemic is guided by an invisible agent that does not leave human blood nor destruction of physical environments in its rapid contamination, human illness and deadly action. The political pressure on experts to establish an immediate solution to neutralize this pandemic is aligned with the greed of the market that privileges the world of darkness. Science's time is different from politics' time. On other hand, this picture has shown the excellence of care, commitment and love of health professionals who have treated patients with covid-19 patients. The high mortality rate of these professionals demonstrates their commitments to the preservation of life. It also shows the negligence of the public authorities with the working conditions of this category.

Grandpa, I remain very optimistic. I believe that this dark phase of the world's sanitary conditions will pass, and social and economic activities will resume at an increasing rate. However, I am sure that, although all the lessons learned by mankind during this painful process strengthen the implantation and historical legitimization of sustainable development, the pains and sufferings of this period of apocalypse pose other challenges for mankind.

I highlight the so-called 'unpredictable civilizing frameworks.' These pictures are very dependent on human feelings, and therefore have a high degree of unpredictability. I present this central question as follows: How to compose the civilizing's structures and systems in progress, which are in process of convivial rupture due to covid-19, with the material and symbolic representations emerging and associated with the new existential practices that will start to guide people's routine. Certainly sustainability is a key element in this process that embraces all mankind. How to eliminate extreme poverty? How to guarantee people full access to public policies? How to live in a multicultural world in a sustainable way? These are broad and challenging issues that we must solve quickly. Grandpa, there are also problems that worry me, before I played with my friends every day in the school playground. What will it be like now? And Grandma? How will she give her dance lessons to her students?

Sustainability's singular dimension refers to its connections with nature and religions. Nature has been a source of aesthetic reference and religious inspiration in every time and place. For religions it is considered a sacred entity, a symbolic condition that constitutes an important and strategic factor for the globalization of sustainability. The meaning of sacred presupposes what must be protected from extinction. It reaffirms the commitment to perenniality of life and the planet, enhancing the secularization of sustainability. The composition of this dimension of sustainability with its humanization will result in new economic and social tensions, because radical environmentalism and exacerbated religious beliefs conspire against a consensual solution, in a world dominated by privatist interests. The future of religions has convergences and tendencies to align the axis of the sacred towards human dignity and the defense of nature. On the other hand, spirit's absolute sustainability is opposed to human beings's biological non-sustainability. Grandfather, this is a very sensitive issue that we must understand better. The connections of sustainability with life and, also, with death must be better researched. I would very much like people to reflect more about this.

In 2100 we will witness sustainable enterprises guiding the splendour of life and the social promotion in the world, on continents, countries, cities, communities and also in families, without exceptions. The gradual and definitive substitution of a civilizing conception based on common sense by another based on science and technology, with full control over cloning technologies, nanotechnology innovations, space platforms with high tech technologies is strategic for the success of full sustainability. The virtualization of information and communication languages and the existence of a human being with a new perception of world and nature, will contribute to the emergence of this global social and economic architecture.

Grandpa, I am particularly concerned with the organization and construction of the sustainable city. Like 'Cities of Calvin,' it represents a human being's ideary to meet himself, with the 'other' and the 'world' in a humanistic and universal perspective. The sustainable city also has this claim, although its existential realization presupposes the establishment of shared democracy. At the organisational level, state-market society must be mobilised to create standard routines and codes for commercial practices, regulating the cycles of movement of sustainable products and consumption.

The concept of a solidary sustainable city presupposes its imbrication to nature and vice versa, breaking with the duality of dominated nature versus protected nature. Its operation prioritizes its forms of occupation, housing and mobility. The choices of educational and technological policies that move its productive and economic flows, the construction of citizenship and cultural processes in a intercultural perspective are determinants to its success.

It is necessary that these dimensions of the cities of the future are integrated with nature in its different concept, valuing the urban environments and considering it and nature as an inseparable whole. This concept requires organizing and preserving large green areas to humanize and integrate these environments. It also requires implementing technological structures that apprehend sustainable development in circumstances that are particular to each village, city and region, and interconnecting the material and symbolic representations of these territories to space-world, reaffirming the expressions of differences and multiculturalities.

These cities spread overflowing geographies, histories and cultural matrices in all dimensions, through a collective ethic connected to education, science and technology. Grandpa, it is crucial that the cities of the future incorporate resilience into its designs, structures and public policies. Resilience to climate change, natural disasters, social and economic conflicts, and forms of organization that weaken the collective and integrative projects are important political dimensions for the construction of sustainable cities. The operational mechanisms of these resiliences will mitigate the effects of the vulnerability of these cities.

The city of the future will require urban planners to compose multi thematic work teams, which apprehend the various dimensions of sustainability, in a systemic and contextualized way to house, residential districts, cities and countries. Soon, interactivity will move cybercities, creating new virtual spaces and symbolic systems that, by transporting the geographies and stories of places and regions, will also be fundamental to legitimize the sustainable practices.

Grandfather, family is one of the main references in people's praxis. Its connections with all the dimensions of the sustainable city should favor the practices that make its realities more humanized and socioeconomically protected.

Finally, I note that the global ecological crisis involves the question of mankind's moral universality. This moral has been disconnected from nature, and the boundaries of politics have ignored the environmental phenomena. I also note that the pollution, greenhouse effect, destruction of the ozone layer, El Niño phenomenon, urban and rural landscapes and the millenary knowledge of indigenous peoples and traditional populations have already been incorporated to the national and international agendas as elements of exchange value. This tendency signals a new global environment economy in the financial markets. At this global juncture, it is important that world institutions are aligned in the defense of cultures and preservation of great world environments, as is the case of Amazonia. UNESCO, the UN, Vatican, business organizations, leaders and world public opinion must define a strategy for the preservation and sustainable use of this strategic region. This cultural and ecological heritage of Brazil and the world needs to be perpetuated.

My dear grandfather, during our great journey through life in the universe, we cannot leave anyone behind. I am optimistic that the deleterious dimensions of sustainability will be eliminated; our future solidarity also depends on this type of synergy.

11. I am very happy with our world

Talking with Loris Malaguzzi (1920-1994), an Italian educator, I better understood his original and fruitful children's education program, still absent in the traditional schools. Program formulated from the students' own ideas and materialized through different languages, having in the art its main cognitive and operational reference. Wisdom, shared learning, construction of civility and the collective world are constitutive elements of this educational approach conceived and implemented by the women of Villa cella, a city in northeastern Italy, after the Second World War. Happiness and transformation are key words in this conception of early childhood education that should overflow all educational systems, integrating the cultural diversities and promoting the common future of all. I am fully identified with this educational concept, because from an early age I learned and decided that the verbs 'smile, trust and share' would move my existence and encourage me to create a healthy and happy life. In a journey in which my self-esteem and self-consciousness will promote the continuous search for originality and creativity in each human being.

My family creates happiness, and it has shown me that it is not a product for consumption, it needs to be continually reinvented because of our relationships with others, with ourselves and with the world... Today I talked with Pope Francis (1936-....), shared his determination and crusade against eugenics and euthanasia, as well as his ecumenical tolerance with the great humanistic transformations in our time. I conveyed to the Pope my concerns about creating peace and a world without borders, and informed him about my dialogue with Barack Obama (1961-....) in 2013, when he was sworn as 44th president of the

United States. At that time, we emphasized the importance of the leadership of the US in this process.

Pope Francis and Barack Obama admit the need for broad agreements with China's President Xi Jinping (1953-...) aimed at creating new political and ecological contracts for the planet. I also spoke with the new President of the United States, Joe Biden (1942-....), who reaffirmed his commitment to these contracts aimed at combating poverty, the planet's intensified ecological depreciation and promoting human dignity.

I also spoke with Jesus Christ, the prophet Mohammed and Buddha about the beauty of the world and the importance of their teachings to universalize human wisdom. We agreed about the need for peaceful coexistence between Christians, Muslims, Buddhists and Jews to create peace and an ecumenical future for all. I smiled with Albert Einstein (1879-1955) when he explained to me the importance of his studies for the development of mankind.

Einstein showed me how he dematerialized the processes of nature by means of languages that geometrize our mental projections of the universe. He explained the relevance of the sciences to socioeconomic development, and cultural and artistic representations. He reaffirmed the relevance of scientific education for the spiritual improvement of people and societies, through two broad interventions: the incorporation of innovations into public policies and the continuous humanization of collective structures.

In 2021 I also talked with Angela Merkel (1954-....), Chancellor of Germany, about the future of unified Europe and her responsibilities facing the major challenges of this century. Social inclusion, sustainable development, covid-19 pandemics and the construction of a new world economic order were the prevalent themes. I listened attentively to Samuel Benchimol (1923-2002), an illustrious professor from Amazonia who showed me that it is possible to enterprise, innovate and preserve the environment from a sustainable perspective, valuing cultures and human dignity. I have had long conversations with anonymous workers; nurses, masons, carpenters, teachers, drivers, mechanics, farmers – ... and also with the homeless. In these meetings we have always shared our hope and confidence in the future.

In November 1971, I had a long conversation with Pablo Neruda (1904-1973), just after he received the Nobel Prize for Literature. We talked about the meaning of his work for mankind and concluded that the world was invented from poetry. On that occasion we revisited his books: Twilight; Twenty poems of love and a desperate song; Attempt of the infinite man; The inhabitant and his hope. Novel; General song; All love; One hundred sonnets of love; Art of birds; End of the world; Garden of winter; and The invisible river. I proposed that his work be musicalized and incorporated into school curricula, so that it can warm the hearts and minds of the citizens of the world. I am convinced that the evils as well as the achievements of the world are historical constructions of subjects, institutions and political powers, so they can be redirected to the common good.

In my conversation with my grandfather, I note that the globalization of the problems of mankind also poses challenges that transcend my generation. The emergence of the Societies of

Wisdom is a singular case, considering that these entities will have a decisive role in the economic and political unification of the planet.

Societies of Wisdom are structures constituted by the integration of a set of enterprises in networks focused on the planet's social and ecological stability. They propose to create a culture of world solidarity, to reaffirm the freedom of expression as the foundation of the civilizing process, and crystallize the technological innovation culture in networks. They will make the transition from the memory societies to the network societies with the availability of knowledge on worldwide scope. They also propose reforming the institutions and the training programmes for teachers and ensuring continuing education for all, defining the future of higher education with an emphasis on new teaching technologies, to the university education market and to construction of new forms of financing education. They take on responsibility in revolutionizing scientific and technological management processes in networks, and create national and international actions directed at human security.

Finally, they propose to ensure universal access to knowledge with emphasis on sharing and the protection of intellectual property, recreate public spaces in new shared structures, and legitimize the paradigm of sustainable development, prioritizing the process of climate change mitigation. These Societies are essential to the success of a sustainable future. Their consolidation requires new conceptual approaches and structures for science and technology, science education, communication, marketing, emphasizing the aesthetics of reception and the notion of sustainability.

I am happy to participate and contribute to these ventures; I am very happy.

12. I want to share my happiness with everyone

There is no definition for happiness, but shared, spontaneous or induced happiness by people presupposes a material and symbolic basis consisting of ethical behaviors and commitments centered on the collective and universal responsibility for everyone's future. Grandpa, people like me, I like them too; in my conception, shared happiness equals responsibilities, commitments and collective dreams. We can create sustainable shared happiness and incrust it in the subjectivity of the dreamers with the better world, spreading it in our educational systems and communication media, virtual and real. I will ask Leonardo da Vinci (1452-1519), Pablo Picasso (1881-1973) and Charles Chaplin (1889-1977) to help us invent a future seated on shared happiness moved by art. A new civilizing dimension with nuances and contours delimited by the shared happiness of mankind, referenced as a portal to other more fruitful realities. Wise human beings create the present looking to the future, with happiness shared in solving universal problems. It does not matter if my shared happiness does not fit in the classical philosophical theories; it is fundamental that it is one of the driving forces of structural changes in behavior and in interpersonal relationships in this increasingly complex world.

Mobilizing world opinion is a key element in this process. Implementing sustainable development models integrated to cultural, ecological and socioeconomic complexities, and committed to regional and national realities is also a task of my generation. Providing social structures and technologies accessible to everyone, generating environmental preservation, income, social value and citizenship for the populations, also enhances this process. If the world really belongs to everyone, then it is possible to create shared happiness.

13. We will be together later

I am tired, Grandpa. I will rest in the Time of Dream – one of the dimensions of time of the culture of indigenous peoples in New Guinea. This Time is constituted of an infinite spiritual cycle, more real than reality itself, which can establish spiritual powers unusual to people. I believe that these powers are driven by sensitivity, and by the set of elements proper to the dynamics of society and the human being's relationship with nature. It is the aesthetics of nature based on the assumption that relationships between human beings and nature also pass through relationships between human beings.

Broadly speaking, the concept of nature involves not only what is external to people, but also what is internal to him with links between the local and the universal, incorporating cosmic sense to human existence. In this reciprocal interweaving, the 'human being-nature' moves to gestate a new history of the world, creating new forms and contents, reinventing the cosmos and with universal thought reaffirming the non-existence of eternal civilization. The thesis that life is a process has been reaffirmed. The idea that nature cannot be conceived without movement, that movement is inseparable from matter, the idea of organic totality and life in all its degrees of complexity, and that nothing in the world is isolated are complex issues of mankind's history. I believe that there is an aesthetic of life that in the postmodernity has privileged the economic and scientific processes.

Grandpa, I also note the importance of two broad positions on the cognitive status of scientific theories in the natural sciences: positivism and realism. For positivists, scientists have the function of inventing laws that describe the phenomena of nature, in the most approximate form possible. Experimentation as a process to legitimize theories, searching for regularity patterns of the research's object and adjustment to theory's conceptual structure used to the statistical methods are structural characteristics of this epistemological conception. Conception that claims to keep nature hostage to human rationality.

The realists take the opposite view, but no less pretentious. They admit, a priori, that the scientist's task is to discover the laws already existing in nature; it is as if nature had a physical existence independent of human beings, obeying laws reducible to physical-mathematical formalism. I understand that these two conceptions are reductionist and deterministic and have the same ontology as matrix: the dissociability between humans and nature. The prevalence of this simplifying scheme of scientific thought continues to pose difficulties in understanding universal history. It also makes it difficult to understand the complexity of life in all its dimensions.

Grandfather, the dissociation between human beings and nature in scientific languages, and the crystallization of the conception of the machine-world contributed to the great technological advancement of mankind. It has also contributed to shifting the notion of 'human condition' to a level of political subordination, eliminating the multiple possibilities of creating a multicultural and ecumenical planetary philosophical perspective. These simplifications have boosted the connection of the natural sciences with the world's economic and political processes. It has contributed to the global spread of the central countries' development models – which are based on the intensified depreciation of nature. This synthesis picture reaffirms the conception in which the universal thought, the culture and the philosophical systems that move western scientific and technological processes are definitely divided into two major strands: studies on the phenomena of nature, considering this entity as an isolated part of human being, and the studies on communities, societies, civilizing processes, finally, on the material and cultural processes that support the organizational and dynamic elements of society, considering them as independent of nature.

The exact sciences isolate human beings from nature, and human sciences isolate the nature of social processes through methodological procedures that strengthen, each one in its own way, the negation of the human being-nature oneness and the refutation of an interdependent epistemic framework.

Intriguing aspect with respect to the cosmic insertion of human beings refers to our material substratum. The cells that form our bodies are made up of atoms that multiply as our biological structure grows. I can say, from the point of view of positivism, that matter is organized and self-organized in the form of atoms. A set of the 118 different types of chemical elements classified in the periodic table that compose the universe's bricks. Its different arrangements have composed the evolution and organizational history of the cosmos since the beginning of its existence 13.7 billion years ago.

I also observe that since the appearance of life on Earth 3.5 billion years ago, during our physical existence, cyclically, flows of atoms of these chemical elements transit between the cosmos and the living being, in both directions, uninterruptedly. This phenomenon occurs during the process of life and death of the human being generations.

This attests, at the limit, the fusion of mankind's history to the universe's history, creating links between creation's past, present and future. This situation shows the fusion of cosmos to the process of life and the life to process of cosmos recreation. This reaffirms the fusion of human condition to nature and to nature in the human condition.

This cycle allows us to incorporate the human condition to the aesthetics of nature, transforming it into aesthetics of life. Aesthetics that also incorporated, definitively, the notion of sustainable development in its existential universe.

Grandfather, I realize that various layers of civilisation that make up the sustainable processes enable this dialogue between the past, present and future of its subjects, as well as the virtuality of being simultaneously in different places and existential times.

Mom, Dad, Grandma and Grandpa, we'll be together later.

14. Good night, Mom, Dad, Grandma and Grandpa

Good night Mom, Dad, Grandma, Grandpa and uncle Lucas, who just arrived. I must sleep after this long journey, because tomorrow, June 25, 2021, after 275 days of pregnancy, I will be born. I would like you to baptize me as Michael. Please, read and publish the poem "Amazonia my love" that I wrote during my long trip. I love you. Grandpa, don't forget, open Mom's bag, Dad's box and Grandma's purse and release the world's history.

15. Amazonia our love

Amazonia our love

Amazonia
Never to be forgotten
Your cultures, your lights, your rivers
Uplift our dreams and delights

Amazonia
For love of your forests
Your birds and animals
Our lives are brighter

Amazonia
Soak our thoughts
With gratitude and generosity
And solidarity for our fellow man

Amazonia
Never to be forgotten

Amazonia

Share your love
With all the peoples of the world
Never abandon the weak

Amazonia
Embrace and comfort
Destroyers of nature
The warmongers
Victims of covid-19

Amazonia
Tell the Amazon river
That he is blessed by the gods
That his waters work miracles

Amazonia
Never to be forgotten

Amazonia
Protect the indigenous peoples
From the ambition and perversity
Worked by the white man

Amazonia
Don't let time
Slip through our fingers
Amazonia, we love you

Recommended reading

"Coronavirus Disease - COVID-19". Nima Rezaei (Editor). Springer Nature Publishing, New York, June 2021.

"Amazonia our treasure" by Marcílio de Freitas. Kindle Direct Publishing – Amazon Book, August 2022.

"Who will save Amazonia: world heritage or full destruction" by Marcílio de Freitas. Nova Science Publishing, New York, July 2021.

"The Future of Amazonia in Brazil; A Worldwide Tragedy" by Marcílio de Freitas and Marilene Corrêa da S. Freitas. Peter Lang Publishing, New York, April 2020.

"The Heavens" by Sandra Newman. Granta Books Publishing, United Kingdom, May 2019.

"A Better Planet; Forty Big Ideas for a Sustainable Future" by Daniel C. Esty. Yale University Press, October 2019.

"The Palgrave Handbook of Sustainability - Case Studies and Practical Solutions". Editors: Robert Brinkmann and Sandra J. Garren. Palgrave Mcmillan Publishing, New York, 2018.

"Prosperity without Growth: Foundations for the Economy of Tomorrow" by Tim Jackson. Routledge Publisher, United Kingdom, December 2016.

"Exhalation: Stories" by Ted Chiang. Knopf Doubleday Publishing, New York, June 2020.

"Heart of Darkness" by Joseph Conrad. Modern Library Publishing, New York, August 1999.

"Silent Spring" by Rachel Carson. Mariner Books Publishing, New York, October 2002.

"The Age of Extremes: A History of the World, 1914-1991" by Eric J. Hobsbawm. Vintage Books Publishing, New York, February 1996.

"The Little Prince" by Antoine de Saint-Exupery, Translated by Irene Testot-Ferry. Wordsworth Editions Publishing, United Kingdom, June 1995.

Made in the USA
Columbia, SC
22 March 2023

14012159R00059